THE

OF HARUHI SUZUMIYA

DISAPPEARANCE

NAGARU TANIGAWA

LITTLE, BROWN AND COMPANY
NEW YORK   BOSTON

Yen
Press

First Published in Japan in 2004 by Kadokawa Shoten Publishing Co.,
LTD., Tokyo. English hardcover/paperback translation rights arranged
with Kadokawa Shoten Publishing Co., LTD., Tokyo, through Tuttle-Mori
Agency, Inc., Tokyo.

English translation by Chris Pai for MX Media LLC

English translation copyright © 2010 by Hachette Book Group, Inc.
Novel translation: MX Media LLC.

Little, Brown and Company

Hachette Book Group
237 Park Avenue, New York, NY 10017
Visit our website at www.lb-teens.com
www.jointhesosbrigade.com

Little, Brown and Company is a division of
Hachette Book Group, Inc.
The Little, Brown name and logo are
trademarks of Hachette Book Group, Inc.

First U.S. Edition: November 2010

The characters and events portrayed in this book are fictitious.
Any similarity to real persons, living or dead, is coincidental and
not intended by the author.

Library of Congress Cataloging-in-Publication Data

Tanigawa, Nagaru.
[Suzumiya Haruhi no Shoshitsu. English]
The disappearance of Haruhi Suzumiya / Nagaru Tanigawa ; [English translation by Chris
Pai]. — 1st U.S. ed.
   p. cm.
"First published in Japan in 2004 by Kadokawa Shoten Publishing Co."
Summary: As the SOS Brigade, a club for a Japanese high school's strangest and most ex-
traordinary students, prepares to celebrate Christmas, Kyon awakens in a weird alternate
dimension and must discover how to set things right.
ISBN 978-0-316-03890-4 (hc) / ISBN 978-0-316-03889-8 (pb)
[1. Supernatural—Fiction. 2. Clubs—Fiction. 3. Space and time—Fiction. 4. Christmas—Fiction.
5. High schools—Fiction. 6. Schools—Fiction. 7. Japan—Fiction.] I. Pai, Chris. II. Title.
PZ7.T16139Dis 2010
[Fic]—dc22
                                        2010009352

10 9 8 7 6 5 4 3 2 1

RRD-C

Printed in the United States of America

```
11001001010010010101010
0100101   010   1010101
010101     0     100101
010010           101010
1010100          1010101
00101001         0100101
111010101      101001010
100101010     010010100
01010101010 01001000101
100101010001010101010
```

NAGARU TANIGAWA

First released in Japan in 2003, *The Melancholy of Haruhi Suzumiya* quickly established itself as a publishing phenomenon, drawing much of its inspiration from Japanese pop culture and Japanese comics in particular. With this foundation, the original publication of each book in the Haruhi series included several black-and-white spot illustrations as well as a four-page color insert—all of which are faithfully reproduced here to preserve the authenticity of the first-ever English edition.

PROLOGUE

It was a frigid morning, so cold that if you poked at the earth with an ice pick, it would probably crack neatly in half. Hell, I felt like doing the cracking myself.

Still, the cold weather was to be expected, since it was winter right now. It'd been rather warm during the cultural festival the previous month, but the second we hit December there was a radical drop in temperature, as if Mother Nature had just remembered what season it was, though as a result I was feeling like autumn hadn't come to Japan this year. That stupid Siberian air mass could try taking a different route every once in a while. You don't have to come our way every single year.

I walked along as I worried about whether the Earth's revolution had gone out of whack or if Mother Nature was feeling under the weather.

"Yo, Kyon."

A frivolous-looking fellow caught up to me and gave me a slap on the shoulder that was as light as hydrogen. It would have been too much of a hassle to stop walking, so I just turned to look at him.

"Yo, Taniguchi."

I replied before turning back to glare at the steep hill stretched out before us. You'd think that our school would cut back on gym class when we have to climb this hill every single day, right? Our homeroom teacher, Okabe, and the other gym teachers should be more concerned about the students, who have to endure the treacherous commute on a daily basis. Especially when they drive to school.

"Why are you grumbling like an old man? Pick up the pace. This is good exercise. Doesn't it warm up the body? Look at me. I'm not even wearing a sweater. The climb may suck during the summer, but it works out perfectly this time of year."

His spunk was nice and all, but where did all that energy come from? Pass some on to me.

Taniguchi's loose lips curled into a grin.

"Finals are over, yeah? Which means there's nothing more to learn this year. Anyway, isn't there a wonderful event coming up?"

All students had to suffer through finals equally. However, the scores on the graded answer sheets were anything but equal.

My mood soured as I recalled my mother fretting over whether she would need to get me a tutor. Next year I would be a second-year, and our class assignments would be determined by the colleges we applied to. Liberal arts or sciences? Public or private? What should I choose?

"Just worry about it later," Taniguchi said with a laugh. "Shouldn't your mind be on other matters right now? Do you know what today's date is?"

"December seventeenth," I said. "What's so special about it?"

"What's so special about it? You've forgotten about the joyous event coming up in a week?"

"Oh, I got it." The answer popped into my mind. "The last day of school is coming up. Winter vacation's certainly an event that's worth anticipating."

Taniguchi glared at me like a small animal encountering a bushfire.

"Hell no! Think carefully about what the date will be in one week. You'll figure it out soon enough."

"Hmph."

I snorted and exhaled a cloud of white.

Oh yeah. December twenty-fourth. Christmas Eve.

Yeah, I knew all about the retail-industry conspiracy coming up next week. I would be the next-to-last person to ever forget about holiday events. Because the last person happens to sit right next to me in class. She was pretty disappointed about missing Halloween a month ago, so she definitely has something planned.

Actually, I already know what she's planned.

This was the exact announcement made by Haruhi Suzumiya in the clubroom yesterday…

"Does anybody here have plans for Christmas Eve?"

Haruhi tossed her book bag aside after shutting the door behind her and glared at us with eyes that shone as brightly as the three stars of Orion's belt.

You could hear an implicit "None of you could possibly have any plans. You people should understand that by now, right?" in her tone, so an affirmative answer would have brought a blizzard down on us.

At that moment I was playing a tactical role-playing game with Koizumi, Asahina was warming her hands by the electric heater in the maid uniform that had become her usual outfit, and Nagato was reading a new science-fiction hardcover without any hint of movement aside from her fingers and eyes.

Haruhi set a large handbag she had also been carrying down on the floor before stomping over to puff up her chest and look down on me.

"Kyon, you certainly don't have any plans, right? I shouldn't need to ask, but I might feel a little guilty if I didn't, so I'm asking now."

She had a smile on her face that reminded me of a Cheshire cat. I handed the dice I was about to throw to Koizumi, who looked at me with a knowing smile, and turned to face Haruhi.

"And what if I do have plans? Why don't you answer that first?"

"Which means you don't have any."

Haruhi determined this arbitrarily as she nodded and turned away from me. Hey, hold it right there, I thought. I didn't answer her question yet…Oh well. This wasn't the first time I didn't have any plans.

"What about you, Koizumi? Going on a date with your girl-friend?"

"If only that were the case."

Koizumi rolled the dice against his palm as he sighed dramatically. A little over the top there, I thought. You're obviously faking it.

"For better or worse, my schedule around Christmas is completely open. I was agonizing over how I might spend Christmas by my lonesome."

His smiling, handsome face was screaming "liar," as far as I was concerned. However, Haruhi instantly believed him.

"There's nothing for you to worry about. You happen to be in luck."

Haruhi proceeded to set a course for the maid girl.

"Mikuru, how about you? Did someone invite you to accompany him late into the night and watch the moment when rain turns to snow? By the way, if you actually run into someone who can still spew that crap with a straight face, you're free to whack him good and hard."

Asahina, staring at Haruhi with her large wide-open eyes, was quivering in response to the abrupt interrogation.

"Well, n-not really. Nothing at the moment…Um, late into the night…? Ah, what about your tea…?"

"Make mine scalding hot. The herb tea from the other day was pretty good."

Asahina immediately responded to Haruhi's order.

"Y-yes! Right away."

Is making tea really that much fun? Asahina's face was shining as she set the pot on the portable gas stove.

Haruhi nodded with a satisfied look before speaking to the last person in the room, Nagato.

"Yuki."

Yuki responded curtly without looking up from her book.

"None."

"Thought so."

That ended the blunt conversation that reminded me of birds chirping. Haruhi turned back to me with a haughty smile on her face. I stared at Nagato's pale face as she kept on reading her book as though she had nothing to do with the transpiring events. You know you don't have to answer her right away. You could at least pretend to try to remember your schedule for a moment or two.

Haruhi raised one hand.

"And there you have it. The SOS Brigade Christmas Party has been unanimously approved. Any objections or protests can be directed to me in writing after the party's over. I'm willing to give them a look-over."

In other words, nobody would be allowed to back out on their commitment, or business as usual. Though I have to admit that she'd made progress over the past six months, since she'd actually asked if anybody had any plans, even if she hadn't intended to take them into consideration. It'd be even better if she asked for our opinions on top of that.

Haruhi, looking satisfied that everything was going according to her plan, reached into the handbag she had dropped on the floor.

"And so, since it's the Christmas season and all, we have a lot of preparations to make, right? So with that in mind, I brought some special items. The proper way to start off one of these events is by creating a holiday atmosphere."

And out came snow spray, gold and silver tinsel, Christmas crackers, a miniature tree, a stuffed reindeer costume, white cotton, Christmas lights, a wreath, a red-and-green curtain, a tapestry depicting the Alps, a windup snowman, fat candles and a candle stand, a huge stocking that a preschooler could have fit inside, Christmas song CDs…

Haruhi smiled like a nice girl passing out candy to the neighborhood kids as she placed the Christmas paraphernalia on the table.

"We're going to spruce up this dreary room. The beginner's method of enjoying Christmas actively and positively starts from the appearance. Didn't you do this when you were a kid?"

When I was a kid? Hell, my sister's room will be Christmas City soon enough. My mom will probably order me to help out again this year. And I should mention that my sister, an eleven-year-old in the fifth grade, still believes in Santa Claus. She still hasn't seen through our parents' clever disguise, the one I saw through early in my life. Knowing my sister's enthusiasm for the holidays, Haruhi chastised me.

"You should learn from your sister's pure heart. You have to have faith to be able to dream. Otherwise, you'll lose what was once within reach. You can't win the lottery without buying a ticket. You can dream all you want about someone giving you the winning ticket for a million dollars, but it's never going to happen!"

Haruhi showed off her ability to yell happily as she pulled out a Santa hat and put it on her head.

"When in Rome, do as the Romans do. You should follow the customs of the place you're in. Christmas has its own set of rules. You won't find many people who would feel upset about having their birthday celebrated. I'm sure that Mr. Christ would be happy to see us having fun!"

I wasn't foolish enough to mention the theories about how we couldn't be sure what year Christ was born, let alone the day. Besides, if I were to tell Haruhi that there were different theoretical dates for the birth of Christ, Haruhi's response would be "Then they can all be Christmas," and she'd force the world to haul out the tree multiple times every year. It's a little late to start arguing about when the AD era began. The solar calendar and the ancient Babylonian calendar were arbitrarily created to suit human needs. The celestial bodies revolving silently around the vast universe certainly won't show any sign of caring before they expire. Yeah, the universe sure has it easy.

Of course, I didn't get a chance to savor this moment of boyhood fascination with the mystery of the cosmos because Haruhi was wandering around the clubroom like a hyper and helpful panda as she placed various Christmas items around the room, set a Santa hat on the head of Nagato, who was buried in her book, and shook the can of snow spray to write the words MERRY XMAS! on the window.

Not that I care, but it's going to look backward from the outside.

In the meantime Mikuru Asahina, with teacup-laden tray in hand, had tottered over like a nutcracker doll.

"Suzumiya, here's your tea."

The sight of the smiling maid Asahina was as fine as always. A fresh balm for my soul every time I see her. It would appear that Asahina, the unfortunate victim whenever Haruhi came up with an idea, showed no concern about the Christmas party. Can't deny that a party with the whole brigade sounds much more enjoyable than passing out flyers in a bunny-girl outfit or wearing a sexually demeaning costume in a movie.

But was that really the case here?

"Thanks, Mikuru."

Haruhi cheerfully took the cup and remained standing as she gulped down the herb tea. Asahina watched her with an angelic smile.

It took Haruhi only half a minute to down the scalding liquid and redouble her smile.

I had a bad feeling about this. She only smiles like that when she's thinking about something dubious. I've spent a decent amount of time with her, so I can notice these things now.

Problem was...

"It was delicious, Mikuru. As a token of my gratitude, I have an early present for you."

"What? Do you really mean it?"

The lovely maid blinked.

"Truer words have never been spoken. True as the moon revolving around the Earth revolving around the sun. You don't have to believe Galileo. Just believe me."

"Ah, y-y-yes."

And Haruhi reached back into her bag.

I felt someone staring at me and turned to meet Koizumi's eyes as he smiled wryly and shrugged. I would have preferred to ask what that was supposed to mean, but I more or less knew what he was saying. We haven't spent the past six months as part of Haruhi's crew for nothing. It'd be pretty wrong if we couldn't figure out what was going on.

At least, that's what I think.

The problem was that there wasn't any person or medicine in this world capable of suppressing Haruhi's ideas. I'll personally present anyone who invents such an item with a Grand Cordon of the Order of the Rising Sun.

"Ta-da!"

With a childish cry, Haruhi pulled out the last of her Christmas items from the bag.

"Th-that's…?"

Asahina reflexively took a step back as Haruhi spoke with the bearing of an old magician passing her beloved staff to her pupil.

"It's Santa, Santa! Isn't it perfect? This time of year, you have to emphasize the season by dressing appropriately. C'mere, I'll help you get changed."

The object in Haruhi's hands as she advanced on the retreating Asahina was, in fact, nothing other than a Santa Claus outfit.

And so Koizumi and I were chased out of the clubroom to fantasize about Haruhi changing Asahina inside.

"Huh?" "Eek!" "Wah!" Her soft shrieks only served as an unneeded boost to my imagination as they gave me the illusion that I could see through the door. Yeah, I think I'm starting to lose it.

After immersing myself in the fantasy for a while…

"I do feel sorry for Asahina."

Koizumi began talking, probably because he was bored. The guy with more than his fair share of looks and bearing leaned against the wall in the hallway with his arms crossed.

"I personally feel very relieved that Suzumiya is having fun. Since it pains me greatly to see her irritated."

"Because that weird space pops up when she's irritated?"

Koizumi used his ring finger to brush his hair aside.

"Yes, that would also be a reason. My comrades and I are most fearful of closed space and <Celestials>. Getting rid of them may have looked like an easy task, but it's actually rather difficult to perform. Fortunately, they've been appearing less frequently since spring."

"Which means they still show up sometimes?"

"Indeed. They still appear on occasion. Recently they've been limited to appearing between midnight and dawn. Probably the time frame when Suzumiya is asleep. I would assume that she unconsciously creates closed space when she has nightmares."

"She makes trouble for everybody, whether she's asleep or awake."

"By no means!"

A surprisingly sharp retort from Koizumi. I have to admit that I was a little surprised. Koizumi smiled thinly as he directed a penetrating look my way.

"You probably don't have any idea about what Suzumiya was like before high school. We began observing her three years before she came to North High, and we never once imagined that she would learn to laugh on a daily basis. Everything changed after she met you—or, to be more exact, after the two of you returned from closed space together. Suzumiya's mental state has stabilized to an extent that cannot be compared to how she was in middle school."

I stared back at Koizumi in silence, since I had a feeling I would lose if I looked away.

"Suzumiya is clearly changing. And for the better. We wish to maintain the status quo here. Wouldn't you agree? She now considers the SOS Brigade to be an irreplaceable assembly. You are here. Asahina is here. Nagato is also necessary. I daresay I might also be included. We are united as one."

According to your people, sure.

"Yes. However, this is by no means a bad thing. Do you wish to see Suzumiya set <Celestials> loose every few hours? This may not be for me to say, but that would be in very bad taste."

I have no interest in seeing that. I never will. I can guarantee it.

Koizumi's expression suddenly changed as his usual ambiguous smile returned.

"I'm relieved to hear that. Speaking of change, Suzumiya isn't the only one who's changed. We all have. You and I, along with Asahina and probably Nagato as well. Any person would have to adjust their mentality after spending time with Suzumiya."

I looked away, but not because he had hit the nail on the head. I hadn't realized that I'd changed, so I wasn't particularly upset about his statement. But I was surprised that he had also noticed Nagato's gradual transformation. The sham of a baseball game, a Tanabata festival that spanned three years, the cave cricket extermination, the murder show on a remote island, a looping summer vacation.... As we went through activity after activity, Nagato's reserved manner and gestures certainly showed signs of change, while minute, from her behavior during our chance encounter in the literary club room when this all began. I wasn't just hallucinating. My eyes are at least as sharp as a homemade telescope. In retrospect, she was already acting odd when we were on the remote island. Also when we went to the public pool and Bon Dance. Even more so when she was pretending to be a magician during the film shoot and taking on the computer society in that computer game. But...

That's a good thing. Haruhi aside, I'd consider this revelation to be far more momentous.

"Organizing a Christmas party would be a small price to pay," said Koizumi, with a smile on his face, "for the sake of keeping our world stable. And if it turns out to be an enjoyable experience, I won't have a single complaint."

I was starting to feel a little ticked off about how I couldn't contradict him.

"It's okay now!"

The clubroom door suddenly flew open, and since I had been leaning against said door, which swung inward, I naturally ended up flat on my back.

"Eek!?"

That voice didn't belong to Haruhi or me. It was Asahina. And it came from directly above me. And since I was sprawled on the floor, I had no choice but to look up at the ceiling, only I saw something else instead.

"Hey, Kyon! No peeping!"

That was Haruhi yelling.

"Wah, whoa!"

That was probably Asahina panicking as she hopped backward. I swear to the gods that I saw nothing but leg.

"Are you going to lie there forever!? Get up!"

Haruhi grabbed my collar as I finally stood up.

"You're such a perv, Kyon! Come back in 200,005,600 years if you want to sneak a peek at Mikuru's underwear! I bet you did that on purpose. You did it on purpose, right?"

It was your fault for opening the door before you even finished warning us. This was an accident. It was an accident, Asahina, I was about to say, when something caught my eye. Anybody want to ask what that something was?

"Wah..."

What else but Asahina standing there with scarlet cheeks.

Red clothing lined in white, topped off by a red hat with a white pom-pom... was all Asahina had on as she gripped her short skirt with both hands and gazed at me with eyes that were teared up from embarrassment.

She made for an utterly perfect Santa without a single flaw. The true identity of this Mikuru Asahina must be that of the grand-daughter who's taken over the family business from a senile old Santa Claus.

I'm willing to bet that eight out of ten people would believe that story. My little sister would certainly fall for it.

"Extremely lovely."

Koizumi offered his impression.

"Forgive my use of a cliché, as I couldn't come up with anything better. Yes, it's very becoming. Yes, indeed."

"Right?"

Haruhi draped her arm around Asahina's shoulder and rubbed her cheek against the flabbergasted Santa girl.

"You're so cute! Mikuru, you should be more confident in yourself. From now until the Christmas party, you'll be the SOS Brigade's very own Santa Claus. You're qualified to hold that position!"

"Eep."

Asahina released a pitiful squeal. Still, Haruhi was actually right for once. Nobody would argue that point, I thought, as I turned to look at Nagato. The petite, short-haired, reticent girl was still reading in silence.

With a Santa hat on her head.

After that, Haruhi had us all line up so she could address us.

"Okay? This time of year, you can't go running after a Santa when you spot one in the middle of town. They're all fakes. The real one only appears at specific locations. Mikuru, you should be especially careful. Don't accept any gifts from strange Santas or agree to anything they ask."

You shouldn't be saying that after you forced Asahina to become a fake Santa.

Don't tell me that someone her age still believes, the way my little sister does, in an old man who volunteers internationally. I suppose it's possible, when she still wishes on falling stars, but I had my doubts. After all, Saint Asahina was blessing us with her presence in the clubroom. Here we had a fake that transcended the original. What's wrong with that? Ask for any more and complaints will come flying in from Scandinavia.

I considered where you might find a shady source of capital for a lazy old man who worked only once a year.

"So, Kyon. We're going to have a full-blown Christmas party and all, but since I just came up with the idea so late, we can only celebrate the birthday of Christ this year. Next year we'll have to hold birthday parties for Buddha and Muhammad as well, or it wouldn't be fair."

Why don't you celebrate the birthdays of the founders of Manichaeism and Zoroastrianism while you're at it? They can only laugh bitterly from their perch above the clouds as a bunch of nonbelievers celebrate their birthdays. And since Haruhi will celebrate anything if it gives her an excuse to go crazy, it evens out in the end. Please limit any potential divine judgment to Haruhi. I barely have anything to do with this farce.

As I tried to figure out which god I should direct my plea to, Haruhi sat down in the brigade chief's seat.

"What would you like? A hot pot? Sukiyaki? No crab. I can't stand that stuff. I get all worked up when I have to pry the meat from the shell. Why aren't crab shells edible? I'm tempted to say that there was a mistake in the evolutionary process."

That's exactly why they have shells. They didn't go through natural selection on the bottom of the ocean for you to eat them.

Koizumi raised his hand before speaking.

"We'll need to place a reservation then. The Christmas season is fast approaching, so we must hurry before all the restaurants are booked full."

I really don't want to go to any place he recommends. We'd be taking the risk of some bizarre restaurant owner character showing up in the middle of dinner to set off another messed-up murder comedy, which actually happened the last time Koizumi suggested an outing together.

"Oh, you don't have to worry about that," Koizumi said.

Haruhi shook her head with a smile. Maybe she was thinking the same thing I was. But she continued.

"We'll hold it here. We already have everything necessary. Just need food. Right, we should bring a rice cooker. And no alcohol allowed. I swore to never drink again."

I can think of some better things for you to swear off, but I believe you just said something that needs to be addressed first.

"Hold it here?" I asked as I looked around the clubroom.

Sure, the room was equipped with a pot and a portable gas stove. And we even had a fridge enshrined. The above items had been brought in by Haruhi from God knows where when the SOS Brigade was first formed. Don't tell me that she'd been preparing for this event. In any case, the stove has proven useful when Asahina's making her special tea, though I have to wonder if we're even allowed to cook on school grounds, especially when we're in the ancient clubhouse. The answer would obviously be no. Fire is banned in the building.

"Sure."

Haruhi paid no heed as she smiled like a grade-schooler who had no certification but cooked like a pro.

"It's more fun to do these things in secret. If any student council members or teachers barge in, I'll treat them to some of my fabulous hot pot. They'll be so overwhelmed by the magnificent taste that they'll tearfully accept the SOS Brigade! That's how it'll go down. To the letter. It's perfect!"

Haruhi is ordinarily loath to engage in any activity that requires effort, but once she's set her mind to doing something, she'll do an extraordinary job of it. Her cooking is probably as good as she says. But a hot pot? When was that decided? From our conversation, her only concern was that we skip the crab. So she pretended to ask for our opinions while deciding everything herself—well, nothing new about that. No point in worrying about it…

That all happened yesterday. I finished giving Taniguchi an abridged rundown of those events as we arrived at our high school.

"A Christmas party, huh?"

Taniguchi passed through the school gate with a half-smile on his face.

"Sounds like something Suzumiya would do. A hot-pot party in the clubroom, eh? Well, you'd better not let the teachers find you. That'll be a pain."

"Why don't you join us?"

I had already told him that we were holding a party, so I gave him an invitation. Haruhi shouldn't have any problem with Taniguchi. He, Kunikida, and Tsuruya make up the trio who fill in when we need some more people.

However, Taniguchi shook his head.

"Nah. Sorry, man. I don't have time to chow down on some lame hot pot that day."

What's with the creepy laugh?

"Now, look here. Only losers who aren't popular gather together on Christmas Eve for a hot pot. I'm sorry to say that I'm no longer one of those men."

Get outta here.

"Right on. I've got a red heart-mark on the twenty-fourth in my planner. Sorry. I feel for you, man. Really, I mean it."

What the hell. While I was busy playing along with the wacky antics of Haruhi and the SOS Brigade, stupid Taniguchi managed to land himself a girlfriend.

"Who is it?" I asked, trying my best to not sound jealous.

"A first-year from Kouyouen. A safe bet, right?"

Kouyouen Academy. The all-girls school in front of the station at the bottom of the hill. It was built at the starting point of our long and painful climb, so I would see girls in black blazers parading by every morning. The place was famous for its rich high-society girls, but I was more envious of how they didn't have to trudge up this killer slope. I mean, I wasn't envious of Taniguchi at all.

"What's your beef? You've got Suzumiya, yeah? A hot pot... She'll be doing the cooking? Though I'm not sure you can call a hot pot cooking, but it'll still fill you up. I'd love to be in your shoes, Kyon."

Jerk. He brought up Christmas Eve because he wanted to brag?

"Well, I need to plan out where we'll be going. Tough decisions to make."

I was dumbfounded. And speechless.

Nothing significant happened after school that day. Koizumi and I were forced to put up the new decorations that Haruhi had brought to the clubroom while she stood and pointed. Asahina was the tea-serving mascot in a Santa outfit. Nagato was silently reading a hardcover with a Santa hat on her head again.

That was it for the day. We didn't decide on the contents of the hot pot. The only apparent decision was that I would be the one to go out and buy everything needed. What kind of hot pot are we going with? I'm really hoping that she doesn't choose something suspect like a potluck…

Well, that was a little long for a prologue. However, everything so far has only been a prologue. The real story begins now, starting with the next day. Though it may have begun tonight. Not that it really matters.

The next day would be December eighteenth, a day cold enough to freeze the wind. The day I was thrown into the abyss known as fear.

Let me make this clear now.

It definitely wasn't a laughing matter.

CHAPTER 1

The next morning I was awoken by the usual combination of my sister ripping off my bedcovers while the calico wormed into my blanket. My little sister, the assassin who dutifully carries out our mother's command every morning.

"Mom said that you should eat breakfast."

My sister smiled cheerfully as she lifted the stretching cat off of my bed and rubbed her nose against the back of its ears.

"Shami's breakfast is also ready."

Shamisen, left in our care after the cultural festival, yawned sleepily as he licked his front paw. The male calico who could formerly talk had lost his voice and established himself as a beloved pet in our household. His transformation into a perfectly ordinary cat made me wonder if I had been hallucinating when I heard him speak in human. He may have also forgotten how to speak in cat, since he barely ever made a sound, which was fine by me. For some unknown reason, Shamisen was sleeping in my room, allowing me to be rudely awoken by the frequent visits from my little sister to play with him.

"Shami, Shami. Time to eat."

My sister sang out of tune as she struggled to carry the cat out of the room. I was getting goose bumps from the frigid morning air as I looked blankly at the time on the clock, but I eventually shook off the desire to linger in my warm bed, and sat up.

Once I finished changing and washed my face, I headed downstairs to the dining room, gobbled down breakfast in five minutes, and exited through the door two steps in front of my sister. It was another bitterly cold day.

Everything had been normal up until this point.

I was climbing up the hill as always when I spotted the back of a familiar-looking head. The figure walking ten meters or so ahead of me was definitely Taniguchi. He normally seemed so energetic as he practically bounced up the hill, but he was unusually slow today. I caught up to him in no time.

"Yo, Taniguchi."

I figured that I should also get to slap him on the shoulder on occasion, so I did just that.

"…Meh. Kyon, huh?"

Taniguchi's voice was muffled, which was to be expected, since he was wearing a white flu mask.

"What's wrong? Did you catch a cold?"

"Ah…?" Taniguchi replied sluggishly. "As you can see, I have a cold. I wanted to stay home today, but my dad was being a pain."

You were perfectly fine yesterday. This cold came out of the blue.

"What are you talking about? I was feeling pretty crappy yesterday. Cough."

I was completely thrown off by the peculiar sight of a subdued Taniguchi as he coughed up a lung. But wait, he was already feeling sick yesterday? I recalled him being his usual conceited self.

"Hmm…really? It sure didn't seem that way to me."

I smirked maliciously at Taniguchi as he cocked his head.

"You sounded so happy as you went on about your plans for Christmas Eve. Well, you'd better recover in time for your date. Opportunities like this one are probably hard to come by."

However, Taniguchi merely cocked his head a little further.

"A date? What are you talking about? I don't have any plans for Christmas Eve." Taniguchi coughed.

And what are you talking about? What happened to your little girlfriend from Kouyouen? Did you get dumped last night?

"Hey, Kyon. Seriously, what are you on? I have no idea what you're talking about."

Taniguchi shut his mouth peevishly and returned his head to a forward direction. I guess he's been hit really hard by the cold symptoms, since he doesn't seem to be faking his infirmity. And judging from his reaction, I probably guessed right when I suggested that his date had fallen apart. No wonder he's all worn out. It must hurt to look at my face after all the bragging he did. I see how it is.

"Don't get too down on yourself."

I patted Taniguchi on the back.

"You up for the hot-pot spectacular? It isn't too late to join in."

"What hot pot? Where is this alleged event going to be held? I haven't heard anything about it…"

Oh, really. I can see that the shock means he won't be hearing anything I say for the time being. I'll just back off in that case. Everything will be solved in the course of boundless and perpetual time. I won't say another word about it.

I joined the plodding Taniguchi in climbing slowly up the hill.

It would have been impossible to notice at this point.

*   *   *

I was surprised to find that the cold had spread through class 1-5 while I wasn't paying attention. I barely made it inside the classroom before the bell rang, yet there were plenty of empty seats, and a fifth of the present students were sporting flu masks. I'm guessing that incubation periods had been synchronized to the point where symptoms showed up for everyone at the same time.

But the real surprise came when first period began and the seat directly behind me was still empty.

"Well, how about that?"

Even Haruhi's sick? Do we have a really nasty cold going around this year? I find it hard to believe that there are pathogens brave enough to invade her body or that Haruhi would lose to bacteria or viruses. I'd be more inclined to believe that she was busy at work on some new crackpot scheme she'd hatched up. Does she have something besides the hot pot in mind?

In any case, the frigid air in the classroom wasn't because of a lack of heating. I didn't expect there to be a sudden epidemic of absent classmates. It almost felt as though there'd been a drop in the population of class 1-5.

The absence of Haruhi breathing down my neck may have been a factor, but the classroom somehow felt like a different place.

And after rambling through class, it was time for lunch.

I pulled the cold lunch box out of my bag, and Kunikida walked over with lunch in hand to sit down in the seat behind me.

"Doesn't look like she's here today. It's okay for me to sit here, right?" he said as he unwrapped the napkin around his Tupperware. I've grown half-accustomed to eating lunch with this guy after ending up in the same class for high school. I looked around for our other lunch buddy, Taniguchi, to find that he wasn't in the classroom. I guess he went to the cafeteria or something.

I turned my chair to the side.

"Looks like a cold epidemic came out of nowhere. Hope I don't catch it."

"Hmm?"

Kunikida turned to me with a quizzical look on his face as he methodically set the container on the spread-out napkin and scrutinized its contents. He was snapping his chopsticks together like crab pincers.

"There were signs that a cold was going around a week ago. It doesn't seem to be influenza, though it might have been better that way. Since there's a vaccine now."

"A week ago?" I asked as I stopped in the middle of tearing into my spinach omelet.

I don't believe that there was anybody doing anything a week ago that would have spread germs. I'm pretty sure that nobody was absent, and I can't recall anybody coughing during class. So a disease had been spreading out of my sight, despite the fact that every student in 1-5 looked perfectly healthy?

"Huh? There were quite a few people absent. You didn't notice, Kyon?"

I had no idea. Is that true?

"Uh-huh, it sure is. It only got worse this week. I hope they don't quarantine the entire freshman class. That would probably cut into our winter vacation," Kunikida said as he carried some seasoned rice to his mouth. "Taniguchi's been looking sluggish the past few days. His dad believes that you can cure a cold by using sheer willpower, so Taniguchi isn't allowed to stay home unless his temperature's over 104 degrees. I'm pretty sure he needs to do something before it gets worse."

I stopped my chopsticks in midair.

"Kunikida. Sorry, but I thought that Taniguchi only started looking sick today."

"Huh, no way. He's been like that since the beginning of the week. He sat out gym class yesterday."

I'm getting confused now.

Wait, Kunikida. What are you talking about? As far as I can remember, Taniguchi was going wild enough in the soccer match during yesterday's gym class to make you wonder if he was on steroids. I know because I was on the other team, trying to slide tackle him. Not because I was jealous of his getting a girlfriend or anything, but I probably would have held back if I had known he would be so sick today.

"Really. Huh? That's funny."

Kunikida cocked his head as he picked out the carrots in his burdock root stir-fry.

"Maybe I was mistaken," he said.

He sounded pretty laid-back.

"Mmm, we'll know once we ask Taniguchi later."

What's going on today? Taniguchi and Kunikida aren't making much sense, and Haruhi's absent. This had better not be an omen of some disaster that inconveniences every human being who isn't Haruhi. My nonexistent sixth sense was sounding an alarm as I felt a chill creep up the back of my neck.

Bingo.

My intuition wasn't too shabby. This was, in fact, an omen of things to come. But my intuition was unable to determine who would be inconvenienced. Every human being who isn't Haruhi…was the wrong answer. Oddly enough, there was only one person who would notice this situation and find it disturbing.

The rest of the world wouldn't be inconvenienced in any way. Because they were completely oblivious to what was going on. They're not going to pick up on something they can't pick up on. As far as they're concerned, the world hasn't changed one bit.

So who was the person inconvenienced by this turn of events?

That goes without saying.

Me.

I was the only one left dumbfounded amid these bewildering circumstances while the rest of the world moved on without me.

Yes, I finally realized what was going on.

It was lunchtime on December eighteenth.

The physical manifestation of my bad omen opened the door to the classroom.

A cheer came from the girls near the door at the front of the classroom. It came in response to the entrance of a classmate. I peeked through the crowd of sailor uniforms to see **that person** arrive in grand fashion.

With book bag in hand, **that person** smiled at the approaching flock of friends.

"Yes, I'm fine now. I went to the hospital this morning to get a shot, and I feel much better. I thought I might come in for the afternoon classes."

That came in response to the person inquiring about recovering from a cold and was delivered with a gentle smile. After a quick joke **that person**, with medium-length hair swaying... slowly...walked...toward...us.

"Oh, I should move."

Kunikida stood up with his chopsticks clamped in his mouth. Meanwhile, I was staring at **that person** as though my vocal cords had been robbed of their ability to speak. Actually, I had completely forgotten to breathe. It felt as if an eternity had passed, despite the fact that only a few steps had been taken. Eventually, **that person** came to a halt right next to me.

"What's wrong?"

The question was accompanied by a puzzled expression and followed by a cliché.

"You look like you just saw a ghost. Or is there something on my face?"

Kunikida, packing up his lunch, was the next target.

"Oh, I'm just going to set my bag down here. Go ahead and eat. I had lunch before I came to school. You can borrow my seat for now."

And true to her word, the female student hooked her bag on the side of the desk before turning back to the ring of waiting friends.

"Wait."

My voice cracked a bit.

"Why are you here?"

That person turned around and gave me a frosty, penetrating look.

"What do you mean? Is there something odd about my being here? Or are you trying to imply that I should have been sick longer? What's that supposed to mean?"

"That's not it. I don't care about your cold. I'm talking about—"

"Kyon."

Kunikida was poking at my shoulder with a worried look on his face.

"You're acting really weird. You haven't been making any sense at all, really."

"Kunikida, you don't have a problem with seeing her here?"

I couldn't take this any longer, so I stood up and pointed my finger at **that person**, who was staring at me with a baffled look.

"Don't you know who this is? It's someone who isn't supposed to be here!"

"…Kyon, it's not very polite to forget the face of a classmate when she's only been absent for a few days. Isn't supposed to be here? She's been in our class the whole time."

I could never forget her. It'd take a lot longer than half a year to forget the face of this wannabe murderer who tried to kill me.

"I know."

That person smiled as though she had just come up with a hilarious joke.

"You were probably nodding off as you ate your lunch. Did you have a nightmare or something? That must be it. Isn't it time for you to wake up?"

A smile spread across her comely face as **that person** turned to Kunikida for support. I was focused on the images that had been burned into my brain.

They were flashing through my mind. A classroom in sunset hues—shadows extending across the floor—a windowless wall—distorted space—the swing of a knife—that unnerving smile—crystal grains, crumbling like sand…

Our former class representative who, after being annihilated in the battle with Nagato, was said to have transferred to Canada.

Ryoko Asakura stood before me.

"You'll feel a lot better after you wash your face. Do you have a handkerchief on you? I can lend you mine."

I grabbed Asakura's arm as she reached into her skirt pocket. She might pull out something that isn't her handkerchief.

"No thanks. Anyway, explain what's going on. Every little detail. I especially want to know why you set your bag down on Haruhi's desk. That isn't your seat. It's Haruhi's."

"Haruhi?"

Asakura frowned as she turned to Kunikida.

"Who's this Haruhi? Was there somebody who went by that name?"

Kunikida's response was yet another reason to despair.

"Never heard that name before. Haruhi, is it? How is that spelled?"

"Haruhi is Haruhi," I grumbled as I was hit by a spell of dizziness.

"You people forgot about Haruhi Suzumiya? How could you possibly forget about someone like that…?"

"Haruhi Suzumiya…Uh-huh, Kyon."

Kunikida spoke slowly in a consoling tone.

"There's no such person in this class. Besides, this has been Asakura's desk since the last time we changed seats. Did you confuse our class with a different one? But I don't recall ever hearing the name Suzumiya before. Can't be a freshman…"

"The name doesn't ring a bell for me either."

Asakura seemed to agree that I needed to get my head looked at as she continued in a gentle, purring voice.

"Kunikida-kun, could you look inside my desk real quick? The student directory should be near the end."

I snatched the small notebook from Kunikida as he pulled it out. I immediately opened it to class 1-5's page. I traced my finger down the list of names for the girls.

Saeki, Sakanaka, Suno, Suzuki…

There wasn't a name between Suno and Suzuki. Haruhi Suzumiya's name had vanished from the student directory. It was as if the pages were asking "Who are you looking for? There's no such person" as I shut the directory and closed my eyes.

"…Kunikida. I have a favor to ask."

"What is it?"

"Pinch my cheek. I need to wake up."

"You sure?"

He pinched as hard as he could. It hurt. And it didn't wake me up. I opened my eyes to find that Asakura was still standing before me with her lips pursed in a semicircle.

Something's going on here.

I suddenly noticed that we had the entire class's attention. Their eyes were all focused on me as though I were an old stray with canine distemper. Damn, why? I haven't said anything wrong.

"Son of a bitch."

I asked the people nearby the following two questions.

Where is Haruhi Suzumiya?

Didn't Ryoko Asakura transfer out?

Their responses were no help. Like they were all in on this together.

"Don't know."

"Nope."

I was starting to feel nausea in addition to the dizziness. I was struck by a jarring disconnect from reality that forced me to put my hand on a nearby desk for support. It felt like a part of my soul had been shattered.

Asakura laid her hand on my arm and leaned in with a worried look on her face. The sweet fragrance from her hair was numbing me.

"You should probably go to the nurse's office. Strange things can happen when you're sick. That must be it. I believe that you're coming down with a cold."

No!

I wanted to scream at the top of my lungs. I wasn't acting strange. This situation was strange.

"Let me go."

I brushed Asakura's hand away as I headed for the classroom door. The vague disconcerting sensation had seeped through my skin and into my head. The sudden cold outbreak, the disparity in my conversation with Taniguchi, the absence of Haruhi's name in the student directory, the appearance of Asakura...huh? Haruhi's gone? Nobody remembers her? How is that possible? Doesn't the world revolve around her? Isn't she the focus of everybody in the universe?

I mentally yelled at my legs as they tripped over each other, leaving me to practically crawl out of the classroom.

Nagato's face was the first thing to pop into my mind. She would be able to explain this situation. The reticent, omnipotent alien android, Yuki Nagato, was always able to provide a solution. I'd be willing to say that Nagato was the only reason I was alive today.

Nagato would know.

She would be able to save me from this predicament.

Nagato's class was nearby. It took only a few seconds to reach without my even having to run. My mind was still a jumble as I opened the door and searched for her small and short-haired figure.

She wasn't there.

However, it was too early to despair. She usually spent lunch in the clubroom reading. It'd be hasty to conclude that Nagato had also disappeared just because she wasn't in the classroom.

Koizumi was the next thing to pop into my mind. The literary club room in the old shack was pretty far away. The second-year classroom where I would find Asahina was also in a different building. It would be faster to go down a floor to 1-9. Itsuki Koizumi, you better be there. I've never been so desperate to see Koizumi's grinning face.

I jogged through the hallway and skipped down the stairs, three at a time, as I made my way to the corner of the building where 1-9 was, praying the entire time for the esper freak to be there.

I passed 1-7's classroom and 1-8's classroom to find myself in front of 1-9's...

"...What the hell is this?"

I finally came to a halt as I turned to look at the nameplates on the wall again. To the left of class 1-8 was class 1-7. And to the right of 1-8 was—

A landing that led to the emergency stairwell.

Gone. Without a trace.

"This is too much, man..."

Forget Koizumi.

Class 1-9 no longer existed.

Wits' end, seriously.

Who would imagine that a classroom could disappear in the span of a day? This was nothing like a missing person. Every member of the class was gone. The school building had shrunk. You couldn't manage that in one night, even with a rush job. Where did the members of 1-9 go?

I was so shocked that I had lost track of time. I have no idea how long I stood there, but a jab to my spine brought me back as I listened in a daze to the voice of a biology teacher who reminded me of the Marshmallow Man.

"What are you doing? Class already started. Return to your classroom."

Guess I was so out of it that I didn't even hear the bell. Nobody else was in the hallway as the teacher's voice rang out from the 1-7 classroom.

I slowly began to move. No more time for confirming the omen.

It had already happened. A person was here who shouldn't be. People who should be here weren't. Swapping Asakura for Haruhi, Koizumi, and everybody else in class 1-9 couldn't be considered a fair trade.

"What the heck?"

If I hadn't gone crazy, the world had.

Who was responsible?

Was it you, Haruhi?

As a result, I wasn't listening to a single word during my afternoon classes. Every voice and sound passed right through my ears without leaving any data in my brain cells. The next thing I knew homeroom was over, and so was class for the day.

I was frightened. Not by Asakura, scribbling away with a mechanical pencil in the seat behind mine, but by the fact that Haruhi and Koizumi weren't at school. I was too scared to even ask other people for confirmation. Every time I heard the words "Don't recognize that name," I found myself sinking deeper into a bottomless swamp. I couldn't muster the energy to lift myself from my chair.

Taniguchi immediately left the classroom with Kunikida, who was probably worried about me, while Asakura walked out with a group of laughing girls. She turned to me as she went out the door with a look of genuine concern for a classmate who wasn't well. That only made my head hurt more. This was wrong. Everything was wrong.

I finally grabbed my bag and stepped into the hallway as I followed the people on cleaning duty out of the classroom.

Either way, this wasn't where I should be after school.

I trudged down the stairs in low spirits and when I reached the first floor, I spotted a glimmer of hope and took off running.

"Asahina!"

Nothing could have made me happier. My goddess/eye-balm was walking toward me. Even better, the baby-faced and well-endowed beauty was accompanied by Tsuruya. I was overwhelmed with joy.

—I'm pretty sure that I should have been a little more careful.

I raced over to the two upperclassmen at an incredible speed and grabbed the wide-eyed Asahina by her shoulders.

"Wah!"

I saw the surprise on her face, but my mouth had a mind of its own.

"Haruhi's gone! Koizumi's been *Drifting Classroom*ed! I haven't checked on Nagato yet, but Asakura's here and the entire school is weird. You are my Asahina, right?"

Slip, slam. That was the sound of Asahina's bag and calligraphy set hitting the floor.

"What? Ah, um. Wait. Er. Huh…"

"I mean, you're the Asahina from the future, right?"

Then came Asahina's response.

"…Future? What do you mean? Could you please let me…go?"

I could feel my stomach turn as Asahina looked at me the way a domesticated impala would look at a wild jaguar. She was clearly frightened. The last sight I ever wanted to see.

As I stood dumbfounded, my arm was twisted upward. I heard some disturbing sounds from my joints. That hurts.

"Hold on a minute, young man!"

Tsuruya was using some kind of ancient martial arts technique on my arm.

"You gotta take it slower. Look, our Mikuru's all scared now."

Her tone was light, but her eyes were like daggers. On a closer look, Asahina was certainly backing away with teary eyes.

"Are you a freshman in the Mikuru Fan Club? Everything has a certain procedure to follow. You shouldn't rush things."

That would be the umpteenth chill down my spine today. My arm was still locked by hers.

"Uh, Tsuruya...?"

Tsuruya stared at me as if I were a complete stranger.

Et tu, Tsuruya?

"Hmm? You know me? And who are you anyway? An acquaintance of Mikuru's?"

I refused to believe my eyes. Asahina hiding behind Tsuruya and staring at me openly while shaking her head.

"I—I don't know him. Um. He must have me mixed up with someone else..."

The year was almost over, but that reaction almost made me pass out, as it basically guaranteed that this year would be a bad one. I can put up with pretty much anything that anyone might say to me, but hearing those words from Asahina was the biggest shock I'd received since the cousin I had a crush on as a kid eloped.

I wasn't mixing up this Asahina with some other person named Asahina. It'd be a different story if this actually were some other Asahina...oh, yeah. There's a way to determine if this is actually the Asahina I know.

"Asahina."

I used the arm that was still free to point to my chest. I must have been really upset considering what I said next.

"There should be a star-shaped mole on your breast around here. There is, right? Would it be possible for you to show me—"

I was socked in the face.

By Asahina. By Asahina's fist.

My words had left Asahina stupefied: her face gradually turned red, and tears began to well up in her eyes before she clumsily delivered a smack straight to my face.

"…Sob."

And with that, she ran off in tears.

"Ah, Mikuru. She's so hopeless. Hey, young man. No more of that funny business. Mikuru's really shy! If you try something again, I'm gonna lay the smack down."

After one last painful squeeze to my wrist, Tsuruya picked up the bag and calligraphy set from the floor and ran after Asahina.

"Hold on, Mikuru—!"

"…"

I could only stare in a daze as a gust of cold wind blew through my mind.

It's all over.

Will I live to see the sun rise tomorrow? I'm pretty sure that once word spreads around school that I made Asahina cry, I'll be jumped by more guys than I can count. I'd do the same if I were in their shoes. I should probably come up with some last words to say.

I was finally out of ideas. I called Haruhi's cell phone and got a "number not in use" message from the operator. I couldn't remember her home phone number, which had been erased from the student directory, along with Haruhi's name. I considered going to her house, but then I remembered that I've never been there. Not very fair when you consider that Haruhi's been to my place, but it's too late now.

The missing class 1-9 aside, I went to the faculty office to ask about where Koizumi and Haruhi might be. A miserable experience. There was no student named Haruhi Suzumiya in any class. And there hadn't been a transfer student named Itsuki Koizumi.

There was nothing I could do.

Where would I find a lead? Was this Haruhi's attempt at an

elaborate game of hide-and-seek? I have to figure out where she's disappeared to. But why would she do that?

I continued to think as I walked. Asahina's blow may have helped, as I'd managed to cool my head down. No point in going crazy right now. This is when you have to stay calm. Calm.

"Please be there," I muttered as I headed toward the only destination left. The last bastion. The final line of defense. If it's fallen, this tale is over. Pulled off the air.

The literary club room in the clubhouse, also known as the old shack.

If Nagato isn't there, I'm completely out of options.

Which is why I was walking slowly and taking my time as I headed to the clubroom. A few minutes later I found myself before the old wooden door with my hand on my chest to check my pulse. My heart was certainly beating at an abnormal rate, but this was a significant improvement over the nervous wreck I had been during lunch. My senses may have grown numb after the chain of bizarre happenings. I'm getting desperate. I'll have to march on blindly while anticipating the worst possible outcome.

I skipped the knocking and threw the door open.

"…!"

And there I saw…

A small figure sitting in a metal chair at the corner of the long table with a book opened before her.

Yuki Nagato, staring at me through the lenses of her glasses, with her mouth open in surprise.

"You're here…"

I sighed in relief as I shut the door behind me. Nagato was silent as always, but I was unable to celebrate. I was well aware of the fact that Nagato had stopped wearing glasses after the incident with Asakura. However, the Nagato in front of me was wearing the same glasses as before. Which reminded me of how much better Nagato looked without glasses. At least, by my standards.

Besides, that expression didn't look right on her face. That would be the look of a girl in the literary club who had just been surprised by a strange guy barging in. Why are you surprised? Wouldn't that be the last emotion to expect from your character?

"Nagato."

I'd learned my lesson from what happened with Asahina, so I suppressed the urge to charge over as I slowly approached the table.

"Yes?" Nagato responded without making a move.

"Answer this for me. Do you know who I am?"

Nagato pursed her lips, pushed the bridge of her glasses up, and remained silent.

I was about ready to give up and search for a monastery to join.

"I do."

Nagato was staring at a spot in the vicinity of my chest as she responded. There was hope. This Nagato might be the one I know.

"I actually know a fair deal about you. Do you mind if I talk for a bit?"

" ... "

"You actually aren't a human but an alien-made organic android. You can freely use magic-like powers. Such as by making a bat that only hits home runs or infiltrating cave cricket space..."

I was already regretting those words as I spoke them. Nagato clearly had an odd look on her face. Her mouth was wide open, as were her eyes, which darted between my shoulders. Nagato's demeanor indicated that she was afraid to look me in the face.

"…That would sum up what I know about you. Was I wrong?"

"I'm sorry."

Nagato's response made me question if my ears were functioning properly. Why an apology? Why would Nagato ever say such a thing?

"I wouldn't know. I only know that you're from class 1-5. Because I see you from time to time. But I don't know anything else about you. This would be the first time I've ever talked to you in this place."

My last bastion collapsed like a tall building built on brittle, weathered sand.

"…Which means you aren't an alien? Do you remember anything about the name Haruhi Suzumiya?"

The word "alien" drew a puzzled tilt of the head from Nagato.

"No," came her response.

"Wait."

Who am I supposed to rely on if Nagato's no good? I'm like a newly born swallow who's been abandoned by its parents. I need her help to stay sane. The way things are going now, I'm gonna snap.

"That's impossible."

No good. I'm about to lose my cool again. My mind was a chaotic mess, with red, yellow, and blue shooting stars flying every which way. I circled around to Nagato's side of the table.

Her pale fingers shut the book. That thick hardcover. I didn't have time to catch the title. Nagato stood up from her chair and backed a step away from me. Her eyes, like two polished black Go stones, were quivering hesitantly.

I put my hand on Nagato's shoulder. I was no longer composed enough to recall my prior blunder with Asahina. I was completely focused on preventing her from escaping. If I didn't grab hold of her now, I feared I would find that every person I had ever known had slipped through my fingers. I didn't want to lose any more people.

I could feel the warmth of her body through her uniform as I spoke to the short-haired girl who was trying to turn away from me.

"Remember. The world changed between yesterday and today. Asakura's here instead of Haruhi. Who was responsible for the substitution in personnel? The Data Overmind? You have to know something if Asakura's back. Isn't Asakura one of your brethren? What's the big idea? You should be able to give me an explanation, even if I can't understand it—"

As you always have, I was about to say, but instead I found myself feeling like I had swallowed liquid lead and it was spreading through my stomach.

Why is she reacting like an ordinary human being?

From the side I could see that Nagato's eyes were shut tight and her pale, porcelain-like cheeks were flushed. Short, staccato pants escaped from her parted lips, and I realized that the slender shoulder I was grabbing was quivering like a freezing little puppy. A trembling voice reached my ears.

"Stop…"

That woke me up. At some point Nagato's back had been pinned against the wall. Which means I had unconsciously cornered her. What am I doing? I'm practically assaulting her. If there were any witnesses, I'd immediately find myself with my hands cuffed behind my back and receiving my punishment from society. A sick idiot who attacked a timid female literary club member while she was alone in the clubroom. That would be me, from an objective perspective.

"Sorry about that."

I put my hands in the air.

"I didn't mean to attack you. I just wanted to check something…"

My legs were about to give out on me. I reached for a nearby metal chair and plopped down like a mollusk. Nagato was still glued to the wall. I suppose I was lucky that she didn't race out of the room.

I looked around the clubroom again and instantly realized that this wasn't the SOS Brigade's secret base. This room only had bookshelves, a few metal chairs, a long folding table, and an old desktop computer that sat on top of said table. It wasn't the cutting-edge machine Haruhi had swindled from the computer society. This one was at least three generations older. It was like comparing a carriage with a high-speed rail.

Naturally, there wasn't a brigade chief pyramid or a brigade chief desk for it to sit upon. No fridge and no garment rack with multiple costumes. None of the board games Koizumi had brought in, no maid, and no Santa's granddaughter. Nothing at all.

"Damn it."

I buried my head in my arms. Game over. If this was somebody's idea of a psychological attack, they'd certainly succeeded. A job well done. So, who was behind this experiment? Was it Haruhi, the Data Overmind, or a new enemy of this world…?

Five minutes or so passed. I pretended to pull myself together as I nervously lifted my head.

Nagato was still glued to the wall as she stared at me with her ebony eyes. Her glasses were a little crooked. Though I should probably have thanked the heavens that she no longer looked at me with fear. That face was what you would expect from someone who had just run into her long-dead brother on the street. At least she wouldn't be calling the cops on me. A small source of relief in this panic.

I was about to ask her to sit down, when I realized that I had stolen Nagato's seat. I'll let her have this chair. Or should I pull out another one for her? Wait, she might not want to sit down next to me.

"Sorry."

I apologized again as I stood up. I grabbed a folded-up metal chair and moved to the center of the room. After confirming that I was a sufficient distance from Nagato, I sat down in the chair and buried my head in my arms again.

This was just an insignificant literary club. The same room I'd seen on that May day when an industrial-robot-like Haruhi dragged me there for my first encounter with Nagato. At the time the room only had a table, chairs, bookshelves, and Nagato. The rest of the crap came later. After Haruhi's "This is now our club-room!" proclamation. Like the portable stove, kettle, pot, fridge, computer...

"Hmm?"

I loosened my grip on my head.

Wait, what was in the room again?

Garment rack, hot water dispenser, teapot, teacups, utensils, an old tape deck...

"No."

I needed to find something from the SOS Brigade hideout that hadn't been in this clubroom before the takeover and was in the room now.

"The computer."

It was certainly a different model. There was only a power cord on the floor, so it probably wasn't connected to the Internet. However, this was the only item to draw my attention. The only anomaly I could spot.

Nagato was still standing. She must have been really worried, considering how she'd been watching me the entire time. But the second I glanced her way, she looked down. Upon closer inspection, her cheeks were still faintly flushed. Ah…Nagato. This isn't you. You would never look away with a flushed face.

I attempted to stand up in a casual fashion so she wouldn't be so wary, futile as it might have been.

"Nagato."

I pointed to the back of the computer.

"Do you mind if I use this for a bit?"

Nagato looked surprised before slowly adopting an expression of confusion. After glancing between me and the computer three times, she took a deep breath.

"Wait."

She awkwardly moved the chair in front of the computer, pressed the power button, and sat down.

A hot cup of coffee would have cooled down to an acceptable temperature for a cat to drink in the time it took for the computer to boot up. After a sound like a squirrel gnawing at a tree trunk came to an end, Nagato began moving the mouse deftly. I would guess that she was moving or deleting files. She probably had stuff she didn't want other people to see. I could understand the sentiment. I didn't want anyone else to see my MIKURU folder.

"Go ahead," Nagato said in a barely audible voice, without looking at me, as she left the seat to stand guard against the wall.

"Sorry about that."

I sat down and stared at the monitor, using every trick I knew to search for the MIKURU folder and the SOS Brigade website file, before slouching in defeat.

"…Nothing, huh?"

I couldn't find a link. There wasn't any proof that Haruhi had ever been here.

I was curious about the data Nagato had just hidden, but I could feel a watchful gaze on my back. All signs indicated that the plug would be pulled the instant I found something I shouldn't.

I stood up.

There weren't any clues on this computer. I wasn't actually interested in the Asahina photo collection or the SOS Brigade website. I was hoping that a helpful message from Nagato might appear, like what happened when Haruhi and I were trapped in closed space. That hope had been crushed.

"Sorry about bothering you."

I bid farewell in a weary voice and headed for the door. I'll go home. And go to sleep.

That was when something unexpected happened.

"Wait."

Nagato drew a sheet of coarse paper from the bookshelf and hesitantly stepped before me. Her eyes were fixed on my necktie knot.

"If you'd like…"

She extended a hand.

"Please take this."

I was handed a blank application form.

Well.

It's a good thing that I've been through so many experiences that made no sense at all, or I'd be running around looking for a shrink right now.

Evaluating the circumstances would lead to the conclusion that either I was cuckoo in the head or the world had gone out of whack. I was now able to guarantee that the former was out of the question, seeing as I'm always mentally sound as I deliver my witty remarks regarding all of creation. Note how I'm able to make light of the situation with my banter. What the hey.

"…"

I pulled a Nagato and shut up. I was feeling pretty chilly and in more than one way. I can only pretend to be cheerful for so long.

Nagato had turned into a spectacled bookworm, Asahina was an unfamiliar upperclassman, and Koizumi was off at some other school, since he had never transferred to North High.

What's going on here?

Am I supposed to start all over again? The season isn't right for that. If this is a reset and I'm supposed to start from the beginning...then I should have been returned to my first day of high school. I don't know who was responsible for pressing the reset button, but it's pretty confusing to change the setting without adjusting the flow of time. Just look at how clueless I am now. I thought that was Asahina's job.

And where is she, anyway? As she goes on with her life without a care in the world while I've been hung out to dry...

Where is Haruhi?

Where are you?

Show yourself. This is stressing me out.

"...Damn, why do I have to look for her?"

Or what, you're no longer here, Haruhi?

Give me a break. I have no idea why I feel this way, but nothing's going to happen until you show up. It's unreasonable to leave me by myself to sigh in melancholy. What are you thinking?

I felt like a slave carrying a gigantic boulder up a slope for the construction of a pyramid as I stared up at the cold, overcast sky from my vantage point in the corridor between buildings.

The application form rustled in my pocket.

I returned home to my room to find Shamisen and my sister inside. My sister was smiling innocently as she waved a rod with a fuzzy head around while tapping at the head of Shamisen, sprawled on the bed. Shamisen's eyes were narrowed, as though he considered this action an annoyance, though he sporadically reached out with a paw to play along.

"Ah, welcome home."

My sister looked up at me with a smile.

"Dinner's almost ready. Time for sup-purr, Shami."

Shamisen also looked up at me, but he immediately yawned and turned to halfheartedly fight off my sister's usage of the cat teaser.

Oh, yeah. I still had these two.

"Hey."

I took the cat teaser and flicked it at my sister's forehead.

"Do you remember Haruhi? Or Asahina, for that matter. Nagato? Koizumi? Do you remember playing baseball with them and acting in the movie?"

"What's that, Kyon? No idea."

I proceeded to lift Shamisen.

"How long has this cat been in our house? Who brought him here?"

My sister's large eyes widened into saucers.

"Um, last month. You were the one who brought him home? Right? You got him from a friend who left the country. Right, Shami?"

My sister plucked the calico from my hands and began rubbing her cheek against it affectionately. Shamisen, with sleepy eyes, gave me a knowing look.

"Hand him over."

I took the cat back. Shamisen's whiskers were quivering with irritation from being treated like an object. I'll reward him with some dried cat food later.

"I need to talk to this guy. Alone. So get out of my room. Right now."

"Aw—I wanna talk with him too. That's not fair, Kyon. Huh?… Talk with Shami? Huh? Really?"

I ignored my sister as I lifted her by the waist and carried her out of my room. After ordering her to stay outside, I shut the door.

"Mom. Kyon's gone funny in the head—"

It wasn't long before I heard my sister shouting a potentially true statement as she headed downstairs.

"Okay, Shamisen."

I sat down cross-legged as I spoke to the valuable male calico sitting on the floor.

"I once told you to never speak again. But you can forget about that now. In fact, it would be very reassuring if you were to speak right now. So, Shamisen. Say something. Anything. You can talk philosophy or natural science or whatever. Doesn't have to make sense. Just talk."

Shamisen glanced up at me with a disinterested look. He must have been really bored, since he started grooming himself.

"…Do you understand what I'm saying? You can't talk, but you can still hear me? Something like that? In that case, stick out your right paw for yes and your left paw for no."

I stuck my hand, palm up, in front of his nose. Shamisen sniffed at my hand for a bit, but as expected, I suppose, he showed no sign of understanding what I was saying and returned to his grooming.

Well, yeah.

He had only ever spoken while we were filming the movie, and only for a short time. He turned back into a normal cat the second we finished. He can only be associated with the verbs "eat," "sleep," and "play," just like any other cat.

I've learned one thing, at least. I'm not in a world with talking cats.

"Duh?"

Exhausted, I fell onto the bed and stretched. Cats weren't talking. Which meant that the anomaly came when Shamisen was talking. Which meant that nothing was wrong now. But was that truly the case here?

I wish I could become a cat. Then I wouldn't have to think about any of this, and I could live true to my instincts.

And there I lay, until my sister came to tell me that dinner was ready.

CHAPTER 2

A frozen December eighteenth came to an end, and another day began.

December nineteenth.

Starting today, classes would be shortened for the remainder of the year. This should have happened earlier, but our principal was angry about losing to our local rival in the national mock exam, so he forced the change while preaching about improving academic performance. That part of history hadn't changed.

The only changes were to my surroundings, North High, and anything SOS Brigade–related, huh? I continued on my trek to school, still caught up in somebody's arbitrary scheme, and arrived to find that class 1-5 had more absentees today. Taniguchi's temperature must have finally hit 104 degrees, since he was nowhere to be seen.

And once again Asakura, not Haruhi, was sitting in the seat behind mine.

"Good morning. Are you awake today? I hope you are."

"More or less."

I grimaced as I set my bag on my desk. Asakura rested her chin in her hands.

"But opening your eyes doesn't necessarily mean that you're awake. You have to recognize what your eyes see before you can begin to understand. How about it? Do you have a grasp on your current circumstances?"

"Asakura."

I gave Asakura's pretty face a hard look.

"Either you really don't remember, or you're just playing dumb, so let's make this clear. Have you ever wanted to kill me?"

Asakura's face clouded in response. She was giving me that look you would give to sick people.

"...It seems that you aren't awake yet. I have some advice for you. You should check yourself into a hospital soon. Before it's too late."

She proceeded to shut her mouth and ignore me as she began chatting with the girl who sat next to her.

I turned back to the front of the classroom, crossed my arms, and glared at the air.

How does this example sound?

Let's pretend that there was this very unfortunate person. Unfortunate in every possible way, subjective or objective, to the point where an enlightened Siddhartha in his later years would be forced to look away from this embodiment of misfortune, unlucky to the core. One day he (or *she* would work, but I'm lazy so *he* will do) fell asleep, as he always did in the midst of misfortune, and woke up the next day to find that the world had completely changed. A world so wonderful that calling it a utopia wouldn't be enough to do it justice. A world where the misfortune in his life had been swept away, and his body and soul were now filled to the brim with joy. He would no longer suffer any further misfortune. In one night, some unknown person had sprung him from hell to heaven.

Naturally, he had no say in the matter. He had been brought here by a stranger whose identity he couldn't possibly guess. He couldn't even manage a guess at the motive. It was likely that nobody knew the answer.

So now, should he be happy about his current situation? The changes to the world had eliminated his misfortune. However, there were subtle differences from his former world, and the cause of the change remained a mystery.

Should he be grateful to the unknown benefactor, after evaluating the situation to determine if he was now happy?

I shouldn't have to tell you that I'm not the person in the example. This story's on a completely different level.

Ah…I must say that I used a poor example. I hadn't felt extremely unfortunate before yesterday, and I certainly didn't feel very fortunate right now.

However, if you ignore the scope of the matter, that example more or less covered my current situation. My nerves had been on a roller-coaster ride for the better part of this year, courtesy of the bizarre happenings associated with Haruhi, but that would no longer be a concern for me, apparently.

However—

Haruhi wasn't here, Koizumi wasn't here, Nagato and Asahina were ordinary humans, and the SOS Brigade had vanished without a trace. No aliens, time travel, or ESP. Forget about talking cats. This is an exceedingly ordinary world.

So?

Which one was a better fit for me? Which one would please me more?

Was I happy right now?

After school, I headed to the literary club room out of habit. If you do the same thing every day long enough, your body will move by itself, a typical example of automatic behavior. The same as how you unconsciously wash yourself in a certain order in the shower, like clockwork.

Whenever class ended I would head for the SOS Brigade and drink Asahina's tea while playing a game with Koizumi and listening to Haruhi's incoherent babbling. Habits are hard to break, even the bad ones, or especially the bad ones, I suppose.

But the mood was a little different today.

"What do I do with this?"

I was looking at the blank application form as I walked. Nagato probably gave this to me yesterday as an invitation to join the literary club. But I don't know why she would invite me. Because there weren't any other members and the club was in danger of getting cut? Still, it was gutsy of her to ask me to join her club after I came out of nowhere and practically assaulted her. I guess that Nagato is still an oddball in this messed-up world.

"Wah."

I was on my way to the clubhouse when I passed by the Asahina/Tsuruya combo again. It pained me to see the lovely upperclassman jump and cling to Tsuruya the second she saw me, so I quickly bowed and left in a hurry. I can't wait to return to drinking Asahina's delicious tea on a daily basis.

*   *   *

This time, I knocked and heard a soft reply. Only then did I open the door.

In the clubroom, Nagato's gaze swept across my facial epidermis before returning to the book before her. The act of pushing up her glasses almost looked like a greeting to me.

"Was it okay for me to come back?"

Her small head bobbed up and down. But her eyes remained focused on the open book and she never looked up.

I dropped my bag and began looking around for something to do, but the desolate room didn't provide much to work with, so I was left to stare at the bookshelves.

They were packed with books of all sizes. There were more hardcover books than paperbacks. I'd have to guess that this Nagato was also a fan of thick books.

Silence.

I should have been used to sitting in silence with Nagato, but under the circumstances it was agonizing. I had to say something or I'd have a meltdown.

"Are these books all yours?"

Her response came immediately.

"Some were here before I joined."

Nagato showed me the cover of the hardback in her hands.

"I borrowed this one. From the public library."

There was a bar code sticker to show that it belonged to the city. The laminated cover reflected the fluorescent light and for a second Nagato's glasses were sparkling.

That was the end of the conversation as Nagato returned to quietly reading her thick book and I was left feeling out of place.

The silence was unbearably suffocating. I grasped for a random topic of conversation and blurted out the first thing that came to mind.

"Do you ever write your own stories?"

A three-quarter beat passed.

"I only read."

Her eyes, hidden behind the lenses of her glasses, darted toward the computer for a moment, an action I didn't miss. I see. That would explain what she was doing before I was allowed to use the computer. I became very interested in reading a story written by Nagato. What would she write? Science fiction, I suppose. She wouldn't write romance, would she?

"..."

It'd always been difficult to start a conversation with Nagato. I could see that it wasn't any different with this Nagato.

I turned back to scanning the bookshelves in silence.

My eyes happened to stop at the spine of a certain book.

The title looked familiar. It was the first book of the long foreign sci-fi series that Nagato lent to me when the SOS Brigade was first established, the book with a scary amount of words. Now that I think about it, Nagato was still wearing glasses when she said, "I'll lend you this," and forced the book on me without waiting for my response. It took two weeks to read the whole thing. Feels like it was years ago. Too much has happened.

Enticed by that curiously fond memory, I drew the hardcover from the shelf. I had no intention of reading while standing when I wasn't in a bookstore, so I just flipped through the pages and was about to put the book back when a small rectangular piece of paper fell by my feet.

"What?"

I picked it up. It was a bookmark with an illustration of a flower. The kind bookstores put in your bag without asking—bookmark?

It felt like the world was spinning around me. Yes...Back

then…I opened this book in my room…And found something just like this bookmark…Then I took off on my bike…I could recite that phrase from memory.

Seven PM. Waiting in the park in front of Kouyou Park Station.

I held my breath as I turned the bookmark over with a trembling hand—and saw a message.

"PROGRAM EXECUTE CONDITION—ASSEMBLE THE KEYS. FINAL DEADLINE—TWO DAYS"

The bookmark that fell from the hardcover book had a message in Times New Roman print, just like the last one.

I quickly spun around and took three steps toward the table where Nagato sat. I stared into her widening black pupils.

"Were you the one who wrote this?"

Nagato tilted her head as she gazed at the back of the bookmark I was holding out. She then turned to me with a puzzled look on her face.

"It resembles my handwriting. But…I don't recognize it. I don't remember writing this."

"…I see. Thought so. Yeah, it's okay. I'd be more worried if you did know what this was. I was just a little curious. Yeah, don't mind me…"

I wasn't paying much attention as I made my excuses.

Nagato.

You did leave a message behind. I've never been happier to see such a cut-and-dried message. Was it safe to assume that this was a present from the Nagato I was familiar with? That this was a hint for dealing with the current situation? I mean, why else would she leave this note here?

Program. Condition. Keys. Deadline. Two days.

…Two days?

Today was the nineteenth. Was I supposed to count two days from now or two days from yesterday, when the world went crazy? Worst-case scenario, the deadline would be the twentieth, tomorrow.

The moment of joyous surprise was wearing off like lava slowly cooling. All I knew was that there was a program, and I would have to assemble the keys to execute it. But what were the keys? Where would I find them? How many were there? Where did I go to trade them all in for a prize?

A flurry of question marks spun above my head before merging into one giant question mark.

Would executing this program return the world to how it was before?

I began pulling books from the shelf and returning them at a fast pace while checking to see if any other bookmarks might fall out. I worked busily under Nagato's startled gaze for nada. There weren't any others.

"This is it, huh?"

Well, if I get greedy and ask for too much, I'll be weighed down and end up right back where I started. It's a waste of time and your life gauge to run around using whatever you can find without settling on a destination. I have to start by figuring out the keys. I'm still a fair distance from the summit, but I'm starting to pick up on the correct direction to go.

I opened my lunch box and set it on the table, after asking for permission, and ate my lunch, opening my mind to potential ideas while sitting diagonally across from Nagato. Nagato kept glancing my way, but I was busy operating my chopsticks in a mechanical fashion to carry nourishment to my brain cells.

Once I finished lunch I was about to ask for tea when I remembered that Asahina wasn't here, leaving me dejected but undeterred from my brainstorming. This was the moment of truth. I couldn't let this hard-earned hint go to waste. Focus on the key, the key. Key, key…

I must have spent two hours in deep thought.

I was growing disgusted with my lack of brains as I began muttering to myself.

"I have no idea."

Besides, "key" is a really ambiguous term. I really doubt she's referring to the kind of key that's used on locks. She probably means key as in "keyword" or "key person," but that leaves a lot of area to cover. I wish she'd offered the option to choose from some extra hints regarding what I was looking for. Was it an item or was it a spoken line or was it something you could carry around? I tried to channel what Nagato had been thinking as she wrote on the bookmark, but I could only recall the sight of her reading some complicated book or delivering another helpful but tedious explanation, the Nagato we knew and loved.

I suddenly had an urge to look diagonally across the table, and found that Nagato wasn't moving, as though she had fallen asleep. And it seemed as though she was still on the same page in her book, though that might have just been my imagination. However, as if to prove that she wasn't taking an afternoon nap, Nagato's cheeks flushed in response to my absentminded staring. This version of the literary club member Nagato appeared to be extremely shy or unaccustomed to other people looking at her.

It was rather refreshing to see a familiar-looking girl react in an unfamiliar way. I deliberately continued to observe her.

"…"

Her eyes were focused on the text in the book, but it was obvious that she wasn't taking in a single word. Nagato's mouth was y

slightly open as she breathed without making a sound and the subtle rise and fall of her chest was becoming more pronounced. Her slender cheeks were growing redder by the minute. To be honest, I found this Nagato to be fairly—no, incredibly—cute. For a moment I was almost tempted to just join the literary club and enjoy a world without Haruhi.

But not yet. It was too early for me to give up. I took the bookmark from my pocket and held it tightly while doing my best to avoid bending it. The fact that this piece of paper had been slipped into this world meant that the Nagato with the Santa hat still had business with me. I felt the same way. I hadn't gotten a chance to try some of Haruhi's hot pot yet, and I had never had enough time to burn the image of Asahina in a Santa outfit into my eyelids. We'd been busy decorating the clubroom so my game with Koizumi had been cut off at the best part. I probably would have won if we'd kept going, so I'd be missing out on a hundred yen the way things stood.

A westering sun was shining through the window as we approached the time when the sun became a giant orange ball on its way to hide behind the school building.

I was getting tired of sitting still, and I wasn't going to be able to squeeze any more beneficial output from my head. I stood up and reached for my bag.

"I'm going home for the day."

"I see."

Nagato shut the hardcover she was reading or not reading and slipped it into her book bag as she stood up. Had she been waiting for me to say something?

With bag in hand, I turned to the figure that appeared ready to stay frozen in place until I took the first step.

59

"Say, Nagato."

"What?"

"You live by yourself, right?"

"…Yes."

She was probably wondering how I knew that.

I was going to ask about her family when I noticed her subtly downcast eyelashes. I recalled the room that barely had any furniture. My first visit had been seven months ago when her cosmic psychobabble on an epic scale had given me a jolt in more than one way. The next visit had come on Tanabata three years ago, and Asahina had been with me that time. The second visit actually came before the first one chronologically, so I obviously got skills.

"How about getting a cat? Cats are great. They always act lazy, but you get a feeling that they can understand what you're saying sometimes. I wouldn't be surprised to see a talking cat. For real."

"No pets allowed."

And with that she fell silent with a wistful flutter of her eyes, but then she took a deep breath that sounded like a swallow slicing through the wind before speaking in a weak voice.

"Coming?"

Nagato was staring at my fingernails.

"Where to?" I asked.

My fingernails heard her reply.

"My house."

After a half rest of silence, I spoke.

"…You're okay with it?"

What was going on here? I couldn't tell if she was shy, timid, or pushy. This Nagato seemed to be in an unstable mental state. Or was the mentality of an average girl in her first year of high school supposed to be as irregular as the light curve of Alpha Ceti?

"Yes."

Nagato began walking as if to escape my gaze. She turned off the lights in the clubroom, opened the door, and disappeared into the hallway.

Naturally, I followed her. Nagato's room. Room 708 in the fancy condominium. I should take a peek in her guest room. There might be a new hint inside.

If I found another version of me sleeping there, I'd immediately wake him up.

Nagato and I didn't say a word on the way back from school.

Nagato looked straight ahead in silence as she descended the hill as though a strong, chilly wind were blowing at her back. I was moving my legs in a businesslike fashion as I stared at the back of her head and the hair that had been ruffled by the gusts of wind. There wasn't anything for me to say to her, and I had a feeling that I shouldn't ask why she had invited me.

After a prolonged period of walking, Nagato finally came to a stop before the usual fancy apartment. How many times have I been here? I've been inside Nagato's room twice, I've been outside Asakura's room once, and I've been to the roof of the building once. At the entrance Nagato inputted the password to unlock the door and walked into the lobby without looking back.

She remained silent as we rode the elevator up. After inserting her key into the door of room 8 on the seventh floor, she opened the door and motioned for me to go inside before she entered.

I stepped in without saying a word. The layout of the room was exactly as I remembered it. A desolate place. The living room had a kotatsu and nothing else. There still weren't any curtains.

And there's the guest room. It should be the room beyond that sliding door.

"Mind if I look inside this room?" I asked Nagato as she walked out of the kitchen with a teapot and teacups. Nagato slowly blinked.

"Go ahead."

"Excuse me for a sec."

The door slid open as smoothly as if it had wheels.

"..."

There was only tatami flooring to be found.

Well, that makes sense. I can't keep going back to the past...

I slid the door back in place and held out my open hands for Nagato, watching attentively. My actions must have seemed pointless. However, Nagato didn't say anything as she set the teacups on the table of the kotatsu, knelt down in a formal posture, and began to pour tea.

I sat down cross-legged across from her. It had been like this the first time I came here. I had downed cup after cup of Nagato's tea for no real reason before listening to her cosmic monologue. That had been back during a particularly hot transition from spring to summer, a world from the current frigid weather. Even my soul felt colder.

We sat face-to-face in silence as we drank the tea. Nagato's eyes were focused downward behind her glasses.

It appeared that Nagato was hesitating, as she opened her mouth and then shut it. She would appear to reach a decision and look up at me before looking back down, a motion that she repeated many times, but finally she set her teacup down and spoke in a strangled voice.

"I have met you before."

And then, almost as an afterthought...

"Outside of school."

Where?

"Do you remember?"

Remember what?

"What happened at the library."

As soon as she said those words, I could hear the gears in my brain begin to turn. The memory of the time I had spent with Nagato at the library surfaced. The first stage of that memorable magical mystery tour.

"Back in May."

Nagato was still looking down.

"You helped me get a library card."

I froze as I was hit by a mental shock.

…That's right. Otherwise you would have never budged from the bookshelves. Haruhi was chain-calling me to get our butts down there and I didn't really have a choice if I wanted to hurry back to the meeting point…

"Hey."

However, as Nagato continued with her explanation, her description of that incident differed from the one in my memory. According to the soft, faltering voice of this Nagato—

Nagato had set foot in the public library for the first time ever around mid-May but she hadn't known how to get a library card. The matter would have been settled by asking a librarian, but the few librarians around were all busy. On top of that, she was a reserved, poor speaker who lacked the courage. Then a male high school student who happened to see her loitering around the counter was unable to stand the sorry sight and offered to handle the entire procedure in her stead.

And that was…

"You."

Nagato turned to meet my eyes for half a second before returning her gaze to the top of the kotatsu.

"…"

That particular ellipsis came from both of us. Silence returned to the living room with no furniture as I ran out of things to say. I couldn't respond to the question of whether I remembered the incident or not, because her memory was oddly different from mine. I had certainly helped her get a library card, but I hadn't simply happened to pass by, since I was the one who had taken Nagato to the library in the first place. I had chosen the library as a place to kill time after giving up on the hopeless magical mystery patrol. It wasn't possible for me to have forgotten the sight of Nagato in her uniform following after me in silence, even when my memory was at the level of an infantile sea anemone's.

"…"

Nagato must have been unsure about how to react to my silence, as she bit her lip despondently, and her slender fingers traced the rim of her teacup. Those fingers appeared to be trembling ever so slightly. Her unease left me feeling disinclined to say anything. In fact, I didn't.

It would have been simple to say that I remembered. I wouldn't necessarily be lying. There just happened to be a few discrepancies. And in this situation, those discrepancies were the big problem at hand.

Why were our memories different?

The alien I knew had run off somewhere else. Leaving only a bookmark behind.

Ding-dong—

The perpetual silence was broken by the bell from the intercom. The sudden sound was enough of a surprise to make me jump while seated. Nagato was probably surprised as well. She turned toward the door with a quiver.

The bell rang again. A new visitor, huh? Still, who in the world would visit Nagato's room? I could see only bill collectors and deliverymen ever showing up.

"..."

Nagato stood up like a spirit who had just broken away from her body and moved to the side of her room without a sound. After pressing a button on the intercom panel, she leaned in to listen to whoever was talking on the other side. And then she turned to me with a look of distress on her face.

She was talking softly into the speaker with phrases like "But..." and "Now's not..." in what was likely an attempt at refusal.

"Hold on," she said in a defeated voice as she glided to the entrance and unlocked the door.

"Oh?"

A girl appeared to force the door open with her shoulder as she entered. "Why are you here? That's odd. Nagato would never invite a boy to her place."

The figure in a North High uniform held a pot in both hands as she deftly pressed her toes against the bottom edge of the door to remove her shoes.

"Don't tell me that you forced your way inside."

And why is she here? I never expected to see your face outside the classroom.

"I'm like a volunteer of sorts. Your presence here would be the bigger surprise."

The beautiful face that burst into a smile belonged to the class representative who sat behind me.

Ryoko Asakura had come calling.

"I made too much. It was hot and heavy to carry."

A smiling Asakura set the large pot on top of the kotatsu. This is the smell you'll find in any convenience store this time of year. The pot contained oden, which had pieces of radish, fish cakes, and boiled eggs stewed in the steamy kelp broth. Had Asakura made it?

"That's right. Anything that I can easily make in large quantities, I bring to Nagato from time to time. If you leave Nagato alone, she'll barely eat anything."

Nagato was in the kitchen grabbing plates and chopsticks. I could hear the clatter of tableware.

"So? Are you going to tell me why you're here? I'm quite curious."

I was hard-pressed to come up with an answer. I was here because of Nagato's invitation, but I didn't know the reason for the invitation. To talk about what had happened at the library? We could have done that in the clubroom. I had only taken her up on the invite because I was hoping for a clue or something about those keys, but I certainly couldn't say that out loud. Asakura'll go back to questioning if I'm okay in the head.

I made something up on the spot.

"Oh, right. I was walking home with Nagato...Yeah, I happen to be considering joining the literary club at the moment. I was walking with her while discussing that very topic. We were approaching this apartment building and our conversation wasn't finished, so I decided to come upstairs. No force involved."

"You join the literary club? Sorry, but you really aren't the type. Do you read books? Or do you write them?"

"I'm wondering if I should read or write. That's all."

Once the lid was removed from the pot on top of the kotatsu, a mouthwatering aroma spread through the room. The boiled eggs floating up and down in the broth were an appetizing color.

Asakura, who had knelt down to my diagonal left, was sending peculiar looks at me. If her glances had had any mass, my temple would have been filled with tiny holes. That was how penetrating her stare felt, though I may have been a little self-conscious. The previous Asakura had turned into a homicidal maniac at one point, but I could see hints of confidence and poise behind this Asakura's biting facade. This oden probably tasted better than anything you could find anywhere else. That only served to put more pressure on me. At the moment I didn't feel very confident about anything. I was running all over the place, pretty much.

Unable to take any more of this, I grabbed my bag and stood up.

"Oh, you aren't going to eat?"

I responded to Asakura's teasing question with a stony silence as I tiptoed out of the living room.

"Ah."

I almost collided with Nagato as she exited the kitchen. Nagato was carrying a stack of plates, chopsticks, and a tube of mustard paste.

"I'm leaving. Since I'm probably being a nuisance."

I bid my farewell and turned to leave when I felt a feather-like tug on my arm.

"..."

Nagato was holding my sleeve between her fingers. A pull with as little force as you'd use to pick up a newly born hamster.

She looked as though she would break down at any moment. Nagato had her head down as her fingertips brushed against my sleeve. Did she not want me to leave? Did she feel that being alone with Asakura would be too suffocating? Though it didn't really matter once I saw Nagato looking so fragile.

"—Or that was the plan, but I'll stay and eat. I'm about to starve to death. I won't make it home if I don't get something in my stomach right away."

Her fingers finally let go. I felt a twinge of regret. Under normal

circumstances you'd never see Nagato express herself in such a straightforward fashion. A very rare occurrence.

I returned to the living room to find Asakura narrowing her eyes and giving me a knowing look.

My taste buds wanted to scream in joy, but deep down I had no idea what I was eating as I focused on stuffing oden down my throat. Nagato was going at a slow pace: it took her three minutes to nibble through a piece of kelp. Asakura was the only one trying to lighten the mood with conversation, as I was limited to vague responses.

After an hour of this bivouac-at-the-gates-of-hell meal, my shoulders were completely stiff.

Asakura finally stood up.

"Nagato, you should put the leftovers in another container to refrigerate. I'll come for the pot tomorrow, so have it ready."

I followed suit. I felt as if the chains had finally been removed from my body. Nagato barely nodded as she walked us to the door with her face down.

I made sure that Asakura was already gone.

"Later then," I murmured to Nagato in the doorway. "Mind if I go to your clubroom again tomorrow? I don't really have any-where else to go after school these days."

Nagato stared at me before flashing…

…a smile, faint but plain to see.

Dazzling.

As we rode the elevator down, Asakura turned to me with a chuckle.

"You like Nagato, don't you?"

I sure didn't hate her. If I had to choose between the two, then sure, I liked her. I mean, there was no reason for me to hate her. She's saved my life before. Right. How could I possibly hate Yuki Nagato after she saved me from your dagger of death, Asakura?

…But I couldn't say that out loud. This Asakura was a different Asakura. The same could be said for Nagato. I was the only one on a different page, since they had all turned into ordinary humans. There was no SOS Brigade.

I'm not sure how my beautiful classmate interpreted my silence as she snorted.

"I guess not. I must have been mistaken. You prefer weird girls. Nagato wouldn't qualify."

"How would you know my preferences?"

"I happened to overhear Kunikida mention it. That's how you were in middle school."

Bastard's making up crap again. Kunikida has no idea what he's talking about. Just ignore him.

"Still, if you intend to go out with Nagato, you'd better be serious about it. Or else I won't allow it. Nagato is more sensitive than she looks."

Why was Asakura so concerned about Nagato? I might have understood if we had been in the old world, where Asakura was Nagato's backup. Well, in the end she went postal and had to be eliminated.

"We live in the same building, after all. I can't bring myself to leave her alone. I always start to worry when I look at her. It makes me feel awfully protective of her, you see?"

Kinda, but not really.

That ended our conversation as Asakura stepped off the elevator at the fifth floor. Room 505, was it?

"I'll see you tomorrow."

Asakura flashed a smile at me as the elevator doors shut.

I exited the apartment building. The night air was as cold as an industrial freezer. The biting winds were robbing my body of its warmth and more.

I considered saying hello to the old landlord for a moment before abandoning that idea. The glass window to his office was shuttered, and the lights were off. He had probably gone to bed.

I would love to do the same. Or at least start dreaming. She was probably capable of entering other people's dreams without even trying.

"You're always making trouble for me whether you're around or not, so you could at least show up when it matters. How about listening to one of my wishes for a change…"

As I talked into the night sky, I was given a sudden jolt as I realized the hateful thought going through my mind. I had an urge to smack my head against a hard surface.

"You gotta be kidding me."

My words formed a white puff that dissipated into the air.

I missed Haruhi.

CHAPTER 3

December twentieth.

On the third morning after the world had gone insane, I woke from my dreamless sleep to get out of bed, once again feeling like I had a dozen 30 mm–caliber bullets in my gut. Shamisen fell from his perch on my covers, where he had been sleeping, to land on the floor, where he stretched himself out. I toed his soft belly as I sighed.

My sister peeked in through the doorway. A look of disappointment appeared on her face once she saw that I was awake.

"Hey, did Shami say anything?"

She'd been pestering me with the same question since the night before last. The answer hadn't changed.

"Nope."

I was rubbing my toes in the cat's soft fur, when my sister grabbed Shamisen and walked off while singing her "Time to Eat" song. Cats have it easy; their job is to eat, sleep, and groom themselves. I'd love to trade places with one for a day. Who knows? He might have an easy time helping me find what I'm looking for.

That's right. I still haven't found the keys. I don't even know what the keys are. Program execute condition. I have to figure something out today, or the world will be stuck this way. Though I'm worried that something worse might happen. Deadline, huh…Why was a deadline set? Was this limited time frame the extent of Nagato's abilities?

With plenty of questions and no answers, I headed for school. The overcast sky had people glancing up to check for flakes of snow. We might have a white Christmas this year. The weather would suggest that we'll have accumulation if it snows. I hadn't been paying attention to how much snow we'd gotten the past few years, but this year's winter was more than cold enough for snow. Haruhi would be happier than a kid in a candy shop as she planned a winter event. If Haruhi were here.

I didn't come across anything attention-grabbing as I climbed the hill to North High like always and reached the 1-5 classroom. I suppose that my lack of willpower had filtered down to my legs, as I barely sat down before the bell rang. Many of my classmates were absent, just like yesterday, but I was pleased to see that Taniguchi was back after one day of rest. He still had a flu mask on, but at least he was in class. I never knew that he was such a big fan of school.

And once again Asakura was sitting in the seat behind me with a knowing smile on her face.

"Good morning."

Asakura delivered the same casual greeting she would offer any person. I merely nodded in response.

Okabe dashed through the door as the bell rang and home-room began.

I'd managed to lose track of what day of the week it was. I wasn't even sure if today's class schedule was the one I remembered or not. I couldn't tell if these were the classes we'd had a week ago. I probably wouldn't have noticed if today's schedule had been switched with yesterday's. So was I the crazy one here? Haruhi Suzumiya never existed to begin with, Asakura was the talk of the class, Asahina was an upperclassman beyond my reach, and Nagato was the only member of the literary club.

This was how things were supposed to be, and the SOS Brigade was a product of my imagination.

Bleh, I'm starting to sound pessimistic.

First period was gym and another soccer match, during which I played the role of a defender who had no intention of guarding the goal. Second period was math, which I barely paid any attention to.

I was sprawled on my desk to cool off a bit.

"Yo, Kyon."

That was Taniguchi. His flu mask was shifted below his chin as he flashed his usual foolish grin.

"Science is up next. The teacher's gonna call on our room today. Give me some help."

You'd be a fool to ask me for help. Shouldn't you already know that we're at the same academic level? I won't know the answer if you don't.

"Hey, Kunikida."

I called out to the other member of their duo as he returned from the bathroom.

"Tell Taniguchi everything you know about sodium hydroxide. He's particularly interested in knowing if it's buddies with hydrochloric acid."

"They should be friends, at the very least. Since you get a neutralization reaction when you mix them."

Kunikida sauntered over and peered into Taniguchi's open textbook.

"Oh, this problem. It's easy. You calculate the answer in moles before converting to grams. You see…"

I felt pretty helpless as I watched a knowledgeable person solve the problem like it was nothing.

Taniguchi kept on nodding as Kunikida reached the climax of his calculations. Right then Taniguchi appeared to lose interest in learning the method. He grabbed a mechanical pencil from my desk and wrote the numbers and symbols, as dictated, into the margin of a page in his textbook.

Once that was finished, he flashed me a peculiar smirk.

"Kyon-boy, I heard from Kunikida during the soccer game. You made a lot of noise two days ago, huh?"

Weren't you here two days ago?

"I was sleeping in the nurse's office during lunch. And I was out of it all afternoon 'cause I felt like crap. I didn't hear about it until today. You were raging about how Asakura wasn't supposed to be here or something?"

"Pretty much."

I flipped my hand to tell him to get lost, but Taniguchi merely smirked.

"I wish I could have seen it. We rarely get a chance to see you yelling and screaming."

Kunikida appeared to remember something.

"Kyon seems to have recovered. Though you were still curt with Asakura. Did something happen between the two of you?"

Any attempt to explain would have them thinking I was cuckoo. So I kept my mouth shut. The logical course of action to take.

"That reminds me, you were saying something about Asakura replacing someone else. Did you find that person? Haruhi, was it? Who were you talking about anyway?"

Could you let it drop already? In my current state I'm jumping reflexively every time I hear that name. Even if it were just a parrot repeating her name, I would jump.

"Haruhi?"

Look, Taniguchi has his head tilted to one side. And then he spoke.

"This Haruhi couldn't possibly be Haruhi Suzumiya, could it?"

That's right. Haruhi Suzumiya…

The bones in my neck made a creaking sound as I slowly raised my head to look up at the dumb look on my classmate's face.

"Hey, Taniguchi. What did you just say?"

"I said Suzumiya, y'know? The psycho girl from East Middle. I was in the same class as her all three years. Heh, I wonder what she's up to now.—So how does Kyon know her? What's that crap about Asakura replacing her?"

Everything went white for a moment—

"Damn bastard! You and your gray hairs!" I shouted as I jumped up. I must have given Taniguchi and Kunikida a scare, as they took a step back in unison.

"Don't talk about my gray hairs. You're the one with hairline issues. Besides, white hair runs in my family. From a long-term perspective, you're the one who should be worried."

Shut up. That's none of your business. I grabbed Taniguchi by his shirt and pulled him so close that my nose almost stuck into his face.

"You know Haruhi!?"

"You bet I do. Hell, I won't be able to forget about her after fifty years. If you're from East Middle and you don't know about her, you'd better get your head checked for amnesia."

"Where?"

I was practically growling.

"Where is she? Where is Haruhi? Where'd she go?"

"What's with you? Where, where, where. Are you supposed to be a broken record? Did you happen to catch a glimpse of Suzumiya somewhere and instantly fall for her? Give up on it. I'm trying to be nice here. She might be fine to look at, but that personality ruins everything. For instance..."

"She drew a bunch of white lines on the school grounds to create weird shapes that made no sense. I'm well aware of that incident. I'm not interested in her past misdeeds. Tell me where Haruhi is right now."

"Kouyouen Academy," Taniguchi said. As readily as if he'd been called on to give the atomic number for hydrogen.

"It's the high school at the bottom of the hill near the station. Well, she was certainly smart. Ended up going to a prep school."

Prep school?

"Kouyouen Academy is a good school? I thought it was a place for rich girls."

Taniguchi gave me a condoling look.

"Kyon, I have no idea what they taught you in middle school, but that school's been coed for a long time. And it's famous in our prefecture for the percentage of graduates who go on to college. It's pretty annoying when there's a school like that in our district."

Taniguchi went on to complain about always being compared to Kouyouen as I released my hold on him.

Why didn't I realize it? I should shoot myself in the head.

I assumed that because Haruhi wasn't at North High, she was no longer in this world. Obviously, I had less imagination than a cave cricket. Next summer when I go to the country to visit relatives, I should join one under the floor for a nice chat.

"Hey, what's wrong?" Taniguchi asked as he straightened his shirt. "Yeah, Kunikida, this guy's still acting funny. Isn't that a bad sign?"

Say whatever you want. I didn't care at the time. I was more pissed at a certain someone than Taniguchi, bashing away, or Kunikida, nodding solemnly.

What an incredible case of hard luck. If someone from East Middle had sat near me, if Taniguchi had been in the classroom during lunch two days ago, it would have been a lot easier for me to find someone who knew Haruhi. Did someone set this up? Show yourself, freak. Let me sock you once. But I'm willing to wait until later. I'm done asking questions. Which means that it's time to take action.

"Where are you going? Kyon? The bathroom?"

I turned as I skipped toward the door to reply to Kunikida.

"I'm leaving early."

As soon as possible.

"Without taking your bag?"

It'll get in the way.

"Kunikida, if Okabe asks, tell him that I'm on the verge of dying after coming down with bubonic plague, dysentery, and typhoid fever. Oh, and Taniguchi."

I expressed my heartfelt gratitude to the lovable classmate with his mouth wide open.

"Thanks."

"Y-yeah…?"

I turned away from Taniguchi, spinning his finger around his ear, as I raced out of the classroom. A minute later I was flying out of the school building.

It was difficult to rush down the slope at a high speed. I was so charged up that I ran with everything I had, to the point where, my heart aside, my legs and lungs were objecting to the abuse. Now that I stopped to think about it, I could have waited for third period to end and still be in time. Kouyouen Academy was probably on a half-day schedule by this point in the year, but I didn't need to arrive until the final bell rang. It was only an hour-long stroll from North High.

I didn't realize my failure until I had finished descending the hill that served as my daily mandatory hiking course and the private high school along a private railway was within sight. I took the silence inside the campus to mean that they were still in class. I checked my watch. Their school couldn't be much different from ours, so it was probably third period. Which means I still had over an hour before the gates would open. I had no choice but to wait empty-handed in this frigid air.

"Or should I break in…"

That's what Haruhi would have done and she would have been able to pull it off smoothly, but unfortunately I didn't have enough confidence to do the same, so I moseyed over to the school gate before making a U-turn. There was a tough-looking security guard standing in front of the closed gate. That's a private school for you. They know how to spend money.

I could have climbed over the fence, but it was pretty tall, with barbed wire strung across the top, so I'd be better off waiting quietly. It'd be all over if I forced my way in and got caught. I really didn't want a game over after making it this far. Unlike Haruhi, I knew when to err on the side of caution.

And so I waited for almost two hours.

I heard the sound of a familiar bell and after a bit students began pouring out of the school gates.

I see. It was just like Taniguchi said. This place was a coed school now. The girls still wore the same black blazers, but the boys mixed in were wearing a more traditional school uniform as they hurried on their way home. It was the opposite of North High, where the boys wore blazers and the girls wore sailor uniforms. Though I had a feeling that there were more girls than boys in the crowd…

"Well, how about that?"

There were a few familiar faces among the boys. They were from class 1-9. I thought they'd all vanished, but they'd actually ended up in this school. It may have been pure coincidence, but I didn't see anybody from my middle school. The people I knew didn't show any signs of recognizing me as they gave me suspicious glances before looking away. They were living in a different history. They might even have been living a happier life than when they were students at North High, since they never had to climb this hill.

I continued to wait. There was a fifty percent chance of running into her here. On the off chance that she had joined a club of some kind or was just lounging around inside, I'd have to play scarecrow until she was finished. Please. Start heading home. And appear before me.

What if there was a different SOS Brigade at Kouyouen Academy, with members to replace me and the others…

That thought made my organs churn. She'd have no more business with Asahina, Nagato, Koizumi, and me. That would reduce me from a minor character to a complete outsider. Anything but that, seriously. Who do I have to pray to? Christ, Buddha, Muhammad, Mani, Zoroaster, Lovecraft, anyone will do. I'm willing to believe any myth or folk legend if it removes this anxiety. I'm willing to join one of those shady cults if that's what it takes. A drowning person will grasp at any straw, even if it leads to his sinking in a swamp. I was finally able to understand that sentiment.

I was consumed by irritation, impatience, and gloom for the next ten minutes or so.

"Whew…"

I wasn't entirely sure of the reason behind that sigh. Why would I express myself in such a clear fashion?

There she was.

A face I wouldn't forget for the rest of this lifetime was mixed in with the crowd of black blazers and school uniforms shooting out of the gate.

Her hair was long. Down to her waist, as long as it had been on the first day of school when she paralyzed the entire classroom with her unexpected introduction. After a brief moment of bemused staring, I counted on my fingers to check what day of the week it was. Today wasn't the day to wear her hair straight. I would guess that she wasn't changing hairstyles in this world.

The Kouyouen Academy students were passing by on my left and right as they shot me annoyed looks. I wonder what they thought of this boy from another school standing still in the middle of the path. Not that I really cared. I didn't have time to care.

I remained frozen in place as I watched the blazer-clad girl approach.

Haruhi Suzumiya.

Finally—I found you.

I couldn't help smiling. Haruhi wasn't the only person I'd found.

The student walking next to Haruhi while engaged in conversation was none other than Itsuki Koizumi, with that smiling face I couldn't stand. I'd managed to net an unexpected bonus.

Were they close enough in this world to go home from school together? If so, Haruhi didn't seem very happy about it, as she appeared to be in the same state as when she had first entered high school, according to my memory. She occasionally turned to give a short response before her head swiveled back to glare at the asphalt.

This was how she used to be. Before she came up with the idea of starting the SOS Brigade, when she roamed the school like an irritated martial artist searching for a strong opponent. It's been so long. This was how Haruhi was back then. Bored with ordinary everyday life and desperate to find something more without realizing that she could create her own fun.

No, I can reminisce later. The two of them were getting closer. They hadn't noticed me yet.

It embarrasses me to say that I couldn't keep my heartbeat from racing. If a doctor had listened to my heart, he'd have heard a punkish two-beat that would have made him rip the stethoscope from his ears. I was sweating in this cold air. I hoped I was only imagining that my knees were trembling. I couldn't be that much of a coward.

—Here they came. Haruhi and Koizumi were right before me.

"Hey!"

I managed to make my voice work.

Haruhi looked up and met my eyes.

Her legs, clad in black socks, came to a halt.

"What?" She shot me a look as cold as the frost in a freezer. Her eyes looked me over before she turned away. "What do you want? And who are you anyway? There's no reason to deal with strange men calling out to me. If you want to pick up girls, try someone else. I'm not in the mood."

I had been expecting this reaction, so there wasn't much of a shock. This Haruhi had never met me before.

Koizumi was also standing there as he gave me a neutral look. His face suggested that he'd never seen me before, so we couldn't possibly be acquainted.

I spoke to Koizumi.

"I suppose this would be our first meeting."

Koizumi shrugged.

"So it would seem. Who might you be?"

"Are you still considered a transfer student?"

"I transferred here in spring…why do you ask?"

"Have you ever heard of an organization known as the Agency, by chance?"

"Agency…you say? Is that supposed to be a name?"

The smile on his face, inoffensive and inane, was the one I knew well. However, his eyes were wary as he watched me. Just like with Asahina. He didn't know me.

"Haruhi."

Haruhi's face twitched as she glared at me with her wide black eyes.

"Who gave you permission to address me by name? What's wrong with you? I don't recall requesting stalkers. Move, get out of my way."

"Suzumiya."

"You're not allowed to use my last name either. Besides, how do you know my name? Did you go to East Middle? That uniform's from North High, right? Why are you here?"

Haruhi turned away with a *humph*.

"Don't bother, Koizumi. Just ignore him. There's no point in wasting time on such a rude jerk. He's just another moron. Let's go."

Why were Haruhi and Koizumi walking home from school together? Did Koizumi take over my role in this world? That thought raced through my mind, but there was something else I needed to be concerned about right now.

"Hold on."

I grabbed Haruhi by the shoulder as she tried to walk around me.

"Let me go!"

Haruhi flung my arm off. Her face was filled with pure rage. But that wouldn't be enough for me to let her go without putting up a fight. My trip here would be for nothing.

"You don't know when to give up!"

Haruhi suddenly crouched to deliver an admirable low kick in elegant form. I felt a sharp pain in my ankle and almost collapsed. I had to restrain myself from writhing around in pain. I managed to stay standing as my mind and body cried out in pain.

"Tell me one thing."

I had no choice but to muster my last bit of courage. If this didn't work, I had no chance. My last hope—the question I was about to ask.

"Do you remember the Tanabata from three years ago?"

Haruhi froze in mid-step as she was about to walk away. Her back, covered by her long black hair, was turned to me as I continued speaking.

"On that day, you sneaked into your middle school to draw a bunch of white lines on the school grounds to make a picture, right?"

"What about it?"

Haruhi turned back to me with a pissed-off look on her face.

"Everybody knows about that. What's your point?"

I chose my words carefully before speaking rapidly.

"You weren't the only one who sneaked into school that night. You were with a guy who was carrying Asahina…a girl on his back, and you had him draw the pictograph for you. It was a message to Hikoboshi and Orihime. The meaning was 'I am here' or something—"

I didn't get a chance to continue.

Haruhi's right hand shot out to grab my necktie and pull as hard as she could. Her fearsome strength pulled me so hard that I went flying forward and my forehead smacked right into Haruhi's hard head.

"That hurt!"

I was about to scowl at her and lodge a complaint when I noticed her glaring back at me. She was right up in my face, staring straight at me with a sharp glint in her eyes. Feels like it's been forever since I've gotten to see Haruhi's livid face.

The girl on the verge of snapping asked me in a puzzled voice, "How do you know about that? Who'd you hear it from? No, I never told anybody about what happened when—"

Haruhi abruptly stopped talking as her expression changed and she focused on my uniform.

"North High…it couldn't be.…Say, what's your name?"

Her hold on me was making it hard to breathe. Stupid girl. But I didn't have time right now to feel nostalgic about the same old Haruhi power. My name. Am I supposed to give my real name, which she hasn't used a single time, or the stupid nickname that's managed to stick?

No, neither would mean anything to her right now. She wouldn't recognize either one of them. In that case, there was only one name for me to use.

"John Smith."

I tried to stay composed as I said it, but I mean, she was practically holding me up in midair. The pain was becoming so unbearable that I was really hoping she'd loosen her grip…but the next thing I knew, the strong pressure on my chest was gone.

"…John Smith?"

Haruhi loosened her grip on my necktie as she stood with a dumbfounded look on her face and her arm frozen in midair. Now, this is a really rare sight. Haruhi Suzumiya had her mouth opened in surprise as though her soul had just been taken by the reaper.

"You? You mean to say that you're that John? The weird high school student…who helped me out…at East Middle…"

Haruhi suddenly staggered back. Her long jet-black hair flew across her face as she swayed before Koizumi grabbed her arm to steady her.

I'd found the link.

Helped you out? I'm pretty sure that I basically did all the work—but I had no intention of wasting time on arguing that point. I had finally found a lead. The one person in this messed-up world who remembered something the way I did.

So it really is you, huh?

The one and only Haruhi Suzumiya.

If this Haruhi had met me on Tanabata three years earlier, this current present would have to be connected to that point. This wasn't a total reset. Asahina and I had traveled back in time three years and returned to the present with Nagato's assistance. That part of history remained. I still didn't know when the world had begun to change, but this world had been the world I knew three years earlier.

What could have happened to leave me the only sane person in this world?

Still, I'd have to wait till later to think about it.

I enjoyed the unusual sight of a speechless Haruhi as I continued to speak.

"I'd like to give you a thorough explanation. Do you have time right now? It's a pretty long story..."

The three of us were walking along when Haruhi spoke.

"I met John Smith twice. Afterward, while I was on my way home, he called to me from behind. What was it that he said... oh, right! Yeah, 'Cheers to saving the world by overloading it with fun with John Smith!' was what he shouted. What was that supposed to mean?"

I never did that. Once I made sure that Haruhi was out of sight,

I woke Asahina up and we hurried off to Nagato's apartment. Was there another John Smith? Still, why did that John Smith have to pick those particular words?

It was almost like he was trying to give Haruhi an unnecessary hint.

"Was it the same guy you met at East Middle?"

"He was far away. And it was dark. I don't remember either of their faces. But in terms of voice and demeanor, yeah, he was similar to you. Plus, he was wearing a North High uniform."

This was getting complicated. I thought I'd found a link, but was it still off?

In any case, we went into a nearby café for the moment. It would have been more appropriate to use the usual café in front of the station where the SOS Brigade always met up, but it was too far away.

"The you I know goes to North High and said the following on the first day of school…"

I introduced myself with my real name, not the silly moniker "John Smith," and began my explanation before our order had even arrived and managed to finish my comprehensive digest by the time our café au lait had cooled down enough to drink in one gulp. The SOS Brigade with its alien, time traveler, and esper. The literary club room.

I made sure to give an extensively thorough explanation of the trip through time on Tanabata, since that seemed to be the most critical part.

I glossed over the stuff about Haruhi's being a god, a time warp, or a girl who had the potential for autoevolution, since I wasn't sure about which one was true. I simply said that Haruhi had this odd latent power, an irregular ability to change the world.

Still, it appeared to have been enough to grab her attention, as she sat in deep thought before finally opening her mouth.

"How were you able to read the alien language I came up with? Though it's true that I meant to say that I am here so show yourselves already."

"There was someone to translate for me."

"Was it the alien?"

"An alien-made human contact–purpose humanoid interface… to be exact, I think."

I told them everything I knew about Yuki Nagato. I first thought her to be a bonus thrown in with the literary club, but it turned out that the impassive bookworm had a surprising secret. I also told them about Asahina, the life-size dress-up doll/mascot/PR machine/clubroom maid who was actually from the future. I'd traveled through time with her to that Tanabata night three years ago. Nagato had taken care of our return.

"So the John I met then was you, huh? Yep, I'm willing to believe that. I see. Time travel, huh…?"

Haruhi stared at me as though she wanted to see what a time traveler looked like before nodding.

She was being awfully reasonable about this. I hadn't expected her to believe me so readily. I mean, back when the two of us did magical mystery searches by ourselves, you didn't believe a word I said when we met up in the usual café.

"That version must have been really stupid. I believe you."

Haruhi leaned forward.

"Because it's a lot more fun that way!" she added.

The familiar sight of a smile blossoming on her face. The first smile I'd ever seen from Haruhi. The hundred-watt smile she'd displayed during English class when she came up with the idea of starting the SOS Brigade.

"Besides, I checked out all the students at North High afterward. I even staked the place out. But I never saw anyone like John. I was a little upset with myself for not paying more attention to what he looked like. Right, you weren't at North High three years ago…"

There were two versions of me at the time. One was living an aimless middle-school life. The other was frozen in time with Asahina in Nagato's guest room.

I figured I might as well tell them about the guy here while I was at it.

"Koizumi over there was an esper. You were a pretty big help. Though you also caused a lot of trouble."

"If what you say is true, I would have to be shocked."

Koizumi was holding his cup elegantly as he gave me a skeptical look.

I turned back to Haruhi.

"Why didn't you go to North High?"

"There wasn't any particular reason. I was a little interested in the place after what happened on Tanabata, but John would have graduated by the time I got there. Besides, I wasn't able to find him. And my middle-school homeroom teacher kept bugging me to go to Kouyouen because of the higher percentage of college-bound graduates. I was getting sick of it so I agreed. Any high school would have worked, as far as I was concerned."

I switched my attention to Koizumi.

"What about you? Why did you choose to transfer to this school?"

"My reason would be the same as Suzumiya's. I chose a school that was appropriate for my academic level. I don't mean to speak ill of North High, but Kouyouen Academy has superior facilities."

Since North High doesn't even have air-conditioning.

Haruhi sighed.

"The SOS Brigade, huh…? That sounds really fun."

All thanks to you.

"If we assume that your story is true," Koizumi interjected with a smug face that attempted to suppress a shrewd smile, "there can be only two possible explanations, given the information you've told us."

That really sounded like Koizumi.

"The first would be that you've moved to a parallel world. From your original world to this one. The second explanation would be that the entire world, aside from you, has somehow changed."

I already considered that.

"However, both explanations leave unanswered questions. In the case of the former, the mystery would be the whereabouts of the other version of you, while in the case of the latter, it wouldn't make sense for you to be the only person left out. It might make sense if you happened to possess some kind of magical power."

Nope. I can assure you of that. I got nothing.

Koizumi shrugged with an irritatingly stylish flair.

"If you have moved to a parallel world, it would be necessary for you to devise a plan for returning to your original world. If the world has been changed, you must find a method to return this world to the way it was. In either case, the fastest way to solve this problem would be to find the person who made it happen. After all, that person would most likely know how to return everything to normal."

Who would there be besides Haruhi?

"I wouldn't know. Invaders from another world may be using the Earth as the stage for their little game. It's entirely possible that an evil-looking enemy character will make an appearance."

It was obvious that he wasn't serious about what he was saying. Koizumi was talking in a clearly insolent tone. However, Haruhi must not have noticed, since her eyes were shining, blazing even.

"I want to meet these Nagato and Asahina people. That's right. I also want to check out that clubroom. I might be able to remember something there if I was the one who changed the world. Right, John? You're fine with the idea, right?"

Well, I guess. I have no reason to object. If she was actually the one responsible for this phenomenon—that's what I wanted to believe—then she might be able to learn something. Nagato or Asahina might remember me as well. If the alien and time traveler came back to their senses, we'd be able to deal with this current situation. And was that John supposed to be me?

"Kyon, was it? Isn't this one a lot better? At least John sounds like a human name. It's found everywhere in Western countries. Who came up with that name? Kyon is such a lame nickname. You must have a lot of people looking down on you."

The name came from an aunt, and my sister spread it around. Still, why does Haruhi's abuse feel so comforting? It hasn't been that long.

"Well, let's get going."

Haruhi paid no heed to the Darjeeling tea she had barely touched as she grabbed her Kouyouen Academy schoolbag.

I figured I might as well ask.

"Now? Go where?"

Haruhi came to a stop and looked down at me before exclaiming in a haughty voice.

"North High, obviously!"

And after that quick announcement, Haruhi skipped out of the café at a power-walking speed. She was so psyched that she could barely wait for the automatic doors to slide open.

Typical Haruhi behavior, which was incredibly reassuring.

You're really something, Haruhi. That's how you always were. Taking action two seconds after you think of something. That's how you're supposed to be. Every time, you would show up at the clubroom after practically kicking the door in to tell us about another decision without warning. Nagato would be the only one who wasn't surprised...

"Shoot."

I glanced at my watch. Class was long over. I'd forgotten about the promise I made at Nagato's apartment last night. I said that I'd go to the clubroom today, except I'm already late. I could picture Nagato sitting dejectedly as she waited all alone for a knock on the door. Hold on. I'll be right there.

Koizumi scooped up the bill on the table.

"You realize that I'll only be paying for Suzumiya and myself?"

If you pay for me, I'll tell you something extra.

"Oh? What might that be?"

I regurgitated the whole spiel he'd given me. An abridged version. The theory about Haruhi's being a god, which involved the anthropic principle. His eagerness to anticipate Haruhi's actions. The charade on the remote island.

I let Koizumi mull over that for a bit before I asked another question.

"Was Haruhi responsible, or is there someone else who's capable of creating this situation? Which do you think is correct?"

"Perhaps, if the Suzumiya you speak of truly possesses godlike powers, she may be responsible."

Since I couldn't think of anyone else. Still, that would mean that Haruhi kept Koizumi by her side while ignoring me, Nagato, and Asahina. This may sound conceited, but I really doubted that Haruhi was more attached to Koizumi than to the rest of us. Or was this another one of Haruhi's unconscious moves?

"I suppose I should feel honored about being selected."

Koizumi chuckled.

"After all, I...yes. I'm attracted to Suzumiya."

"...Are you sane?"

You must be joking.

"I find her to be a charming person."

I've heard that line before.

Koizumi continued in a serious voice. "However, Suzumiya is only interested in my classification. She only spoke to me because I was a transfer student. And since I'm an ordinary transfer student, she's begun to lose interest in me. What was your classification in the SOS Brigade, I believe it was called? If you didn't have one, that would mean that Suzumiya was truly fond of you. Assuming that your Suzumiya has the same personality as the one I know."

There's nothing on my record to indicate that I belong in an institute. Besides the useless ability to get dragged into weird stuff without realizing it.

Haruhi stuck her head through the door with a dazzling smile on her face as she shouted.

"What are you doing? Hurry it up!"

After waiting for Koizumi to pay the bill for our drinks, I took the first step out of the warm and comfortable café and into the cold outdoors.

There was a taxi stopped in front of the café. It seemed that Haruhi had flagged it down. She must have been in a real hurry to get to North High. I should mention that it wasn't the familiar black taxi that Koizumi and I occasionally rode in. It was a normal yellow cab.

"North High. Step on it!"

The words were out of Haruhi's mouth before she even sat down in the car. I followed suit, and Koizumi was the last to climb into the backseat. The middle-aged driver didn't show any signs of being upset about a little girl's ordering him around. He smiled wryly and slowly stepped on the gas pedal.

"There's nothing wrong with going to North High," I said from my spot next to Haruhi, "but you're going to stand out in those clothes. A student from a different school needs some kind of reason to get inside. There could be a problem if a teacher spots you."

Haruhi was wearing a black blazer, while Koizumi was in his traditional uniform. Class had been shortened that day, so there wouldn't be many students left that afternoon. Still, these two were going to stick out like sore thumbs when mixed in with the sailor uniforms and navy blue blazers.

"You have a point…"

Haruhi spent three seconds in thought.

"John, did you have gym class today? No, it doesn't matter. Did you leave your gym uniform in the classroom?"

We happened to have soccer during first period today.

"So you have your gym uniform and tracksuit?"

Yeah, but why does it matter?

Haruhi had a satisfied smile on her face.

"I'll tell you my plan. John, Koizumi, huddle up."

Did it really matter if the taxi driver heard us? Either way, we huddled up as Haruhi whispered her so-called plan.

"Sounds like something you'd do," I replied as Koizumi's brow creased with a look of discomfort.

I got out of the cab and headed for my classroom to prepare for Haruhi's plan for infiltrating North High.

Incidentally, the taxi fare was picked up by Koizumi. It seemed that he served as Haruhi's wallet in this world. That's pretty rough when you consider how it isn't necessary punishment. Is this guy seriously romantically interested in Haruhi? I'd love to ask what he sees in her, but I do recall Taniguchi's mentioning that she was popular in middle school, despite her bizarre behavior. Well, it's entirely possible that Haruhi would have shot down a whole parade of potential suitors at North High if she hadn't started the SOS Brigade. In that case, the SOS Brigade served as an effective layer of defense. Her role as the leader of our bizarre club would convince most guys with common sense to avoid her the way a batter would avoid a wild throw. I'd much rather take a walk than strike out or get hit by a pitch.

By the time I finished with that line of thought, I had reached the top floor.

There weren't many people in the building, but at the same time it wasn't entirely empty. I could see a few people here and there who had nothing to do at home or no club activities to deal with. Fortunately, there wasn't anyone in class 1-5, which reminded me that I'd be in trouble if homeroom teacher Okabe found me. If he found out that I had come crawling back after leaving early without permission, he'd surely have some questions for me.

Someone, I don't know who, had helped tidy up my desk. It might have been Asakura. The pencils and notebooks I'd left out had been neatly placed inside the desk, while my bag was hanging from the side. The items I sought were on the other side.

"She comes up with some crazy ideas."

An expression of admiration for Haruhi as I grabbed my gym clothes. This large bag held the short-sleeved shirt, shorts, and tracksuit I'd used during first period. The plan that Haruhi had told us in the taxi on the way here was to "disguise them as North High students," a very logical course of action. "Koizumi can wear your gym uniform, while I wear the tracksuit. Then we can just jog straight in. They'll think that we're members of a sports team that just returned from a run. Yep, perfect."

So basically we're using camouflage, the way insects do. This was obviously a better idea than attacking a boy-girl couple on their way home from school to steal their uniforms.

"That would also have worked."

Haruhi commented casually from the corner outside school where she was waiting. She took the bag of gym clothes from me.

"In fact, that would make it harder for them to pick us out. You should have told us about your excellent idea earlier."

That'd be like committing highway robbery.

Haruhi loosened the cord on the bag and dumped the contents without a smidgen of self-restraint. Four articles of clothing plopped onto the asphalt.

"You washed them, right?"

About a week ago.

"By the way, Suzumiya," Koizumi said.

He was looking at my muddy gym uniform the way a cornered Mongolian gerbil would look at a Mongolian tiger.

"Where do we change? I hope that there's a walled-off space in the vicinity."

"We can change here."

Haruhi replied casually as she picked up the track pants.

"There aren't any people walking by, though it's pretty cold. Oh, don't worry. I'll turn around. You too, John. You can serve as a wall."

What was that sidelong glance supposed to mean?

"I don't mind if you want to watch."

And with a mischievous grin she stepped into the track pants and pulled them up under her skirt.

"My legs shouldn't be that long."

She knelt down to fold up the legs of the pants before standing back up and unfastening her skirt. Then she dropped the skirt without any hesitation, removed her black jacket, and began unbuttoning her blouse, which was when I looked away.

"It doesn't matter. I'm wearing a T-shirt underneath."

I caught the blouse being thrown on top of the jacket and skirt out of the corner of my eye and turned back. Haruhi struck a triumphant pose in a plain white T-shirt and my track pants, with her long hair blowing in the wind. As I watched her, I suddenly recalled a certain sight that I kind of wanted to see again.

"Hey, you up for going ponytail?"

Haruhi gave me a blank look.

"Why?"

No real reason. Just an issue of personal preference.

Haruhi snorted, though she didn't seem to have a problem with the idea.

"It may look simple, but it's actually difficult to do a ponytail correctly."

As she talked, Haruhi reached into the pocket of the black jacket on the ground, pulled out a hair rubber band, and began deftly tying her long black hair behind her head.

"Well, I look more like an athlete this way. Is that good enough?"

Perfect. Your charm has gone up thirty-six percent in my eyes.

"Stupid."

Haruhi always pretends to look angry when she doesn't know how to react. I've learned well.

A short time later Koizumi finished changing. He must be pretty cold wearing a T-shirt and shorts in this weather. And it must feel especially odd to wear someone else's gym uniform. Koizumi had goose bumps popping up as he spoke.

"Suzumiya, you aren't going to wear the tracksuit jacket? In that case, may I borrow it?"

Haruhi's arms were also bare, but she had a smile that appeared to blow the cold away.

"That won't work. I'm using it to hide our bags. It'd be pretty lame if we were caught because of our bags after going through the trouble to disguise ourselves."

The Kouyouen Academy book bag was certainly different in appearance from the North High one in a subtle way. Haruhi wrapped the jacket around their bags and ordered me to carry them. Their discarded uniforms went into my gym bag. I was also ordered to carry that.

"Okay then," Haruhi said.

She placed both hands on her hips.

"We're going to run like we just returned from a marathon. Got it!?"

Sure, I guess. What about me, though? Why would a member of a sports team be out running in his school uniform and carrying all this stuff?

"We'll say that you're the manager. Hey, fight! One, two, fight! One, two..."

I exchanged a glance with Koizumi before shrugging and taking off after the racing ponytail.

This Koizumi and I were both well aware that it was utterly impossible to stop Haruhi once she took off racing, whether literally or figuratively. Which meant that we had no choice but to follow after her.

Right? Isn't that how it always is?

For better or worse, the North High school gate was always open, unlike at the private school at the bottom of the hill. There wasn't a security guard in sight. We passed through without any problems as the short staged marathon with Haruhi shouting came to an end and we reached the goal line, the entrance to the building. I had never thought that inviting Haruhi and Koizumi to my school would be such a pain. Until three days ago, you both walked through this doorway on a regular basis.

"Pretty shabby-looking school. Weren't these walls prefabricated? Are prefectural schools really poor? It's a good thing I didn't apply for this school."

I listened to her reasonable observation as I turned away from the shoe locker. Once I finished changing to my indoor shoes, I began looking around for a pair or two of guest slippers that might happen to be lying around, but Haruhi had no qualms about opening a nearby locker and withdrawing indoor shoes belonging to some unknown North High student.

Her behavior was classic Haruhi, which might have been the reason I had a creepy smile on my face without realizing it.

"What are you smiling about? You look really dumb. I didn't do anything funny."

I dropped the smile. She had a point. Haruhi's craziness was one thing, but this wasn't the time to be smiling.

I threw Taniguchi's shoes to Koizumi, since I figured they'd be about the right size.

"I appreciate it."

Koizumi sure didn't sound very appreciative as he put the shoes on. I stuffed his discarded sneakers into Taniguchi's shoe locker.

I readjusted the bundled jacket with their bags under my arm.

"I'll show you the way. Follow me."

"Hold on."

I was about to step forward when Haruhi stopped me. Her fingers were entwined in the tip of her ponytail, unconsciously, I guess.

"The alien known as Nagato is in the literary club?"

At this point she'd be the high school student formerly known to be an alien. Still, she was probably waiting all alone for me to show up.

"That Nagato is unlikely to run away from us. We should secure the time traveler, Asahina, first. Where is she?"

She probably went home already...but then I remembered. I guess I still have some inspiration left in me. I didn't need to jog my memory much. The Asahina who said she didn't know me had been carrying a calligraphy set, right? And she had belonged to the calligraphy club before she was abducted into the SOS Brigade. In that case, she should still be there at this very moment.

"Got it. This way."

Sorry, Nagato. Hold on a little longer. We have to drop by the calligraphy club first. I prayed for there to be a calligraphy club meeting today as I gradually began to pick up the pace.

Haruhi was the one who opened the door to the clubroom. She didn't understand concepts like modesty or knocking on the door and I didn't have the time to instruct her on how to be polite. Koizumi was standing out in the hallway with an uncomfortable look on his face.

There were three girls in the calligraphy club room, and they appeared to be practicing for New Year's.

"Which one is Asahina?"

The conspicuously smaller member of the three wide-eyed girls answered in an unsure voice. "…Yes? What do you want…?"

Asahina was seated in a chair with a brush in her hand, which was frozen in midair.

I looked over Haruhi's shoulder to check the room. I was relieved to find that Tsuruya wasn't around. I guess she wasn't in the calligraphy club?

Haruhi was whispering into my ear.

"That's her? Is she really a second-year? She looks like she's in middle school."

"I would agree, but that's her. She is most definitely Mikuru Asahina."

Upon hearing that, Haruhi stomped over to tell lies to the petite angel who was frozen in place with brush in hand.

"I'm Suzumiya, head of the student council intelligence service. Mikuru Asahina, we have a few questions for you. We'll need you to come with us for a moment."

How can you say that with a straight face when you're wearing a T-shirt and track pants?

Asahina was blinking rapidly as she spoke in an uneasy voice.

"Student council…intelligence service? What is that…I haven't done anything…"

"Don't worry. Don't worry."

Haruhi grabbed Asahina's brush and placed it on the sheet of paper before grabbing her arm and pulling her up. The other members were either scared or shocked, since they didn't say a word. We may have witnessed an epic battle involving different martial arts if Tsuruya had been around, but Haruhi secured her arm around Asahina and took her away without waiting for a response.

"Hmm…You've got a great body. Yep, plenty of character. I like you."

Haruhi sounded pretty happy as she checked out the upperclassman from another school.

"Eep! Wah, um…ah!?"

Asahina's eyes widened further when she noticed me waiting by the door. She was probably shocked to run into that sicko again. She also looked at Koizumi in surprise as he rubbed his hands together in the hallway to stay warm. Koizumi glanced at Asahina without any sign of recognition.

"I'm actually not a suspicious person. Honestly."

You can't pretend that you're not involved after coming all this way in that getup, Koizumi.

Haruhi was holding on to the struggling Asahina like a mother holding back a child trying to run away from a trip to the dentist.

"Come on, John. Only that Nagato person is left. Take us to her."

Don't need you to tell me that.

We needed to make our way there before I got spotted by a sharp-eyed classmate or teacher who knew about my unauthorized escape.

To the third floor of the clubhouse, also known as the old shack, where we would find the SOS Brigade headquarters, officially known as the literary club room.

I knocked on the door before opening it this time.

"Yo, Nagato."

A spectacled face looked up from the hardcover library book she was reading, which was on the table.

"Ah…"

Nagato sighed in relief when she saw me.

"Huh?"

Then her eyes grew wide upon seeing Haruhi walk in behind me.

"…Eh?"

Her jaw dropped when she saw Haruhi drag Asahina in.

"…"

By the time Koizumi walked through the door, she was speechless.

"Hello," Haruhi said with a smile as she checked that everyone had entered the room before locking the door. Nagato and Asahina both reacted the same way, jumping in response to the click of the door.

"What is this?"

Asahina was almost in tears, just like before.

"Where are we? Why did you bring me here? Why are you l-locking the door? What are you…?"

Her practically identical reaction almost brought tears to my eyes. Ah, the memories.

"Be quiet."

Just as before, Haruhi laid down the law as she looked around the room.

"Is the girl with glasses Nagato? Heya! I'm Haruhi Suzumiya! The guy in the gym uniform is Koizumi, and the little girl with a big chest is Asahina. And you know this guy, right? John Smith."

"John Smith…?"

Nagato pushed her glasses up with a dubious look on her face as she gave me an incredulous glance. I shrugged and accepted the dumb nickname. There wasn't much difference between Kyon and John.

"Hmm, so this is the place. The SOS Brigade, huh? Room's pretty empty, but it's nice. Plenty of space for bringing stuff in."

Haruhi paced the entire length of the clubroom, like a cat checking out her new digs, as she peeked out the window and studied the contents of the bookshelves before she finally turned to me.

"So, what do we do now?"

You came all the way here without a plan? You really are Haruhi, huh?

"I'm all for making this clubroom our base, but the commute's inconvenient. It'll take time to come here after school's over. Our school and North High don't have much interaction. Right, why don't we choose a time to meet up at the café in front of the station?"

Her sudden outburst wasn't making any sense to the other people in this room, excluding me.

Nagato was frozen like a doll with a look of confusion on her face, Asahina was cowering while making strange motions, and Koizumi was opting for silence.

I was about to say whatever first came to mind when—

Beep.

Out of nowhere, the computer my hand was resting on made a sound. Nagato reflexively turned her head.

"Eep?"

I was barely able to notice Asahina's legs giving out on her. The rest of my situational awareness was focused wholly on the computer.

The old CRT monitor flickered audibly as it slowly brightened. I could see the light reflected in Nagato's glasses.

The hard drive began whirring, as though in response to the monitor—but it didn't last long. This has happened before…No, I actually pressed the power button that time…I've been through an experience where the computer failed to boot up, but something still showed up on the monitor…

"Move over a sec."

My body moved by itself. I pushed Haruhi aside as I circled around at full speed to the front of the monitor.

Words were silently appearing on the dark gray screen.

YUKI.N> By the time you read this message, I will no longer be myself.

…Yeah. That's right, Nagato…

"Whoa? Nobody turned the power on. This is a real surprise."

"It may have been set to a timer. Nevertheless, this is quite an ancient computer. It's virtually an antique."

I wasn't listening to Haruhi's and Koizumi's conversation behind me. I couldn't afford to miss a single letter, a single word. No time to blink. I could hear my heart tap dancing as I stared at the screen.

YUKI.N> If this message is on the screen, you, me, Haruhi Suzumiya, Mikuru Asahina, and Itsuki Koizumi must all be standing there.

The cursor scrolled along in a plain font at a speed that almost seemed to match my reading speed.

YUKI.N> Those are the keys. You have found the answer.

I didn't come up with the answer. Haruhi was the one who came crashing in with Koizumi in tow. This Haruhi can also make herself useful... Still, Nagato, haven't seen you in a few days.

I felt a little warm and fuzzy as I read the words on the monitor. I didn't read them out loud, but in my heart I could hear every word in Nagato's quiet voice. The cursor continued to scroll.

YUKI.N> This is an emergency escape program. If you wish to execute, press Enter. Otherwise, press any other key. Once the program is executed, you will be given a chance to correct space-time. However, success is not guaranteed. Neither is your safe return.

Emergency escape program. This. This computer.

YUKI.N> This program can only be executed a single time. Once it starts, it will be deleted. If you have chosen not to

```
run the program, it will delete itself
without executing. Ready?
```

That was it. The blinking cursor sat at the end of the line.

Enter key or any other key, huh?

I turned to find Haruhi peeking at the screen from behind me.

"What does this mean? Is there some kind of trick involved? John, were you just teasing me? Explain yourself."

I ignored Haruhi, Koizumi, and Asahina. I didn't have time to look at Haruhi with a ponytail or Koizumi in my gym uniform or Asahina, cute as always. My focus was on the computer and one single person in this room. I turned to the spectacled girl with a look of surprise on her face.

"Nagato, do you know anything about this?"

"...No."

"You really don't?"

"Why?"

I wanted to reply to her denial of any involvement by saying that she was the one who had typed this message...but that would only confuse this Nagato.

I reread the last part again.

A message left by Nagato. The Nagato I knew. I didn't understand what an emergency escape program did exactly. The stuff about no guarantee was a little unnerving.

However, it was too late to start worrying about that stuff. Nagato had my full confidence. She still has my full confidence. She would never do anything that was a mistake. I mean, we're talking about Yuki Nagato, the docile and soft-spoken alien-made organic humanoid interface who's saved me from danger so many times. I would question my own head before I questioned her words.

"Hey, John. What's wrong? You have a funny look on your face again."

Even Haruhi's voice sounded distant.

"Shut up for a second. I need to organize my thoughts."

Time to think. Haruhi and Koizumi going to a different high school, an Asahina who wasn't from the future, a Nagato who knew nothing at all. I once again realized that those weren't the issues I should be concerned about.

Nagato had expressed herself on the monitor. There was no reason for me to doubt her message.

I stretched and took a deep breath.

Yes—

There was one thing I knew for sure. I wanted to get out of this world. I missed the SOS Brigade, the members of the SOS Brigade, who had become a part of my everyday life. The Haruhi, Asahina, Koizumi, and Nagato here weren't the ones I knew. There would be no Agency or Data Overmind or visits from a grown-up Asahina. That's just wrong.

It didn't take very long for me to make up my mind.

I drew a crumpled-up piece of paper from my pocket.

"Sorry, Nagato. I'll have to return this."

Nagato's pale fingers slowly stretched out to receive the blank application. She failed once before successfully grabbing hold. I released my grip and the application form began to quiver, despite the absence of any wind.

"I see..."

Even Nagato's voice was quivering as her eyelashes concealed whatever emotion her eyes might hold.

"However," I said in a rush, "I was already a resident of this room to begin with, quite frankly. There isn't any need for me to join the literary club. After all—"

Haruhi, Koizumi, and Asahina were looking at me as though I had a few screws loose. Nagato's face was hidden by her hair so I couldn't tell. Doesn't matter. Don't worry, Nagato. No matter what happens next, I'll be sure to come back to this clubroom.

"After all, I'm SOS Brigade member number one."

Ready?

Okay. Bring it on.

I reached out with my finger and pressed the Enter key.

Immediately afterward—

"Whoa?"

I was hit by an intense spell of dizziness as I reached out for the table to steady myself. And then everything began spinning around me. My ears were ringing. I could hear the distant sound of somebody speaking. Growing darker. I've lost my sense of up and down. It felt like I was floating. Like a leaf caught up in the wind. Spinning round and round. The voices calling to me grew more distant. What are they saying? John? Kyon? I couldn't tell. It sounded like Haruhi's voice, but not quite. Dark. Was I falling? Where? Falling where?

My mind was a jumbled mess. Were my eyes open? I couldn't see anything. I couldn't hear anything now. It felt like I was drifting along. Where was my body? What about Haruhi? Everything's distorted. Koizumi. Asahina. Where am I? Where am I going? Emergency escape program. Where will the escape lead me?

Nagato—

"Whoa!"

I cried out again as I practically shattered my knees. Then I noticed that I was standing up.

"What...?"

My surroundings were dark, but not completely dark. It was okay. I could still see.

"This is…"

I used the faint light from the window to check my location. This was a room of some sort and my hands were on a table. There was an old computer on the table…

"The literary club room."

Where I had just been.

But Nagato wasn't there. Haruhi, Asahina, and Koizumi had also disappeared. I was alone. And it was pitch-dark. The room had been illuminated by the setting sun a moment ago, and now it was suddenly the middle of the night. I looked out the window to a very small number of twinkling stars. Time must have zipped by.

The room didn't look much different from before. Bookshelves, a table, and one ancient computer. That was when I realized. I hadn't returned to the original world. None of the SOS Brigade stuff was around. No brigade chief desk or Asahina costume collection. Just an empty literary club room…but…

A drop of sweat from my forehead got into my eye. I used the sleeve of my blazer to wipe it away.

Something was wrong.

Why did something feel wrong? I knew where I was. This was certainly the literary club room. Taniguchi's line suddenly came to mind: Are you supposed to be a broken record? Where? That wasn't the question here. Yes. "Where" wasn't the problem.

"This is…"

I suddenly realized why something felt wrong. As soon as I came to that realization, my body temperature shot up like a rocket, or that's how it felt at least, but that wasn't it. The temperature had been like this to begin with. This wasn't a hallucination caused by a sudden spike in my body temperature.

I couldn't take the heat anymore so I took my jacket off. Pores all over my body began releasing sweat. I removed my sweater and rolled up the sleeves of my shirt and the pent-up heat in the room was still too much for me.

"It's hot," I muttered.

"Almost like—"

Almost like it was the middle of summer.

Which meant there was one question I should be asking.

When was I?

CHAPTER 4

If you've ever walked through a school at night, you know how creepy it feels.

I slung my jacket over my shoulder as I slipped out of the clubroom. I tried to avoid making any sound as I descended the stairs, acting all ninja-like, and slowly checking every corner before moving on. That really tired me out mentally. I still didn't know when or where this North High was, but I knew I couldn't be seen by a teacher on night watch. I wouldn't be able to explain myself. I'm the one who needs an explanation.

The humid air had me sweating as I made my way through the building before I finally reached the entrance.

"Well, what's going to happen now...?"

And with that, I opened my shoe locker to find that it contained someone else's indoor shoes. They certainly weren't mine. I immediately dismissed the possibility that someone had placed his shoes in the wrong locker. It was the middle of summer. I'd been sent to a different space-time. My mind was able to connect the dots. In this world or time, this shoe locker was someone else's, not mine. I wasn't as surprised as I should have been, either because I'd grown accustomed to weird stuff happening or because I was numb after everything I'd been through.

"Guess I don't have a choice."

I didn't have time to gripe about how lame I would look if I went outside wearing indoor shoes. I needed to get out of the school building. The school entrance was locked securely at night, as expected. I made my way to a nearby window, unlocked it, and opened it very carefully. I could smell grass on the night breeze as I placed my foot on the window frame and jumped through to land on the paved ground. I was near the spot where Haruhi had woken me up when we were in closed space.

After ten seconds of staying still, I made sure that no one was watching and began to move.

It was just as hot outside. A smothering, humid heat that was typical of summer in Japan. I'd just come from a frigid winter so my sweat glands were in full gear. I used the winter blazer to wipe the sweat dripping from my face as I headed for the school gate.

It was a simple job to climb over the gate while avoiding the iron spikes, which had me thanking our school's sloppy security. Once I landed outside school grounds I picked up the jacket I had thrown over beforehand and stared at the stars as I planned my next move.

First I needed to figure out what month, what day, and what time it was. There was a huge difference between its being the past or the future.

I figured I might as well start on my way down the hill. There should be a convenience store on the way. A high school student bursting into someone's home to ask what day it was would probably be reported to the proper authorities. So I should probably head for a place where I could learn the time and date.

"Still, it sure is hot..."

I was basically stuck wearing winter clothes and my legs were all sweaty, which made those long pants very uncomfortable. I really hated the inventor of polyester at this point. Besides, this uniform didn't feel that warm in the winter. Seriously, this was one half-assed uniform.

This line of thought suggested that my mind had recovered its ability to function properly. Personally, I'd prefer fanning myself in the summer heat as I griped to waiting in the winter chill for spring to come. Besides, my first summer as a high school student had been a memorable one. Though I'd been exhausted, drained, and disgusted at times, in retrospect, they had all been pleasant experiences. I even got to see Asahina in a swimsuit. The SOS Brigade hasn't done any winter activities yet.

I spent the fifteen-minute descent thinking about how the hot pot might have tasted before I finally spotted the light I'd been looking for. The convenience store I occasionally dropped by on my way home to buy a snack. So I could at least be sure that I'd been sent to a time that wasn't before the store first opened or after it went out of business.

I impatiently waited for the automatic doors to slide open, and as soon as I stepped inside I looked up at the wall. It took a while to get used to the feel of air-conditioning. In the meantime I stared at the analog clock on the wall.

Eight thirty.

PM obviously, since it was night.

What about the date, then? What year, month, and day was it? An assortment of newspapers was on display before the counter. Any one would do. I pulled out a sports paper that happened to be in front and spread it open super-fast. I didn't care about headlines. I'm pretty sure that even a shameless tabloid wouldn't be printed with a fake date at the top of the page.

My eyes darted around before locking on a spot, which was when I saw it...

A set of identical numbers universally considered to be lucky.

From what year? I carefully checked the number on the paper. The guy behind the counter was giving me an irritated look. I couldn't care less.

I kept rechecking the four-digit number. I subtracted the year on the sports paper from the year of the December I had just come from. Simple arithmetic. A child could do it.

"So that's how it is, Nagato..."

I looked up from the newspaper and sighed deeply as I looked up at the ceiling.

Tanabata Day, celebrated nationwide.

It was July seventh, three years ago.

Tanabata three years ago. What happened on this day?

On the Tanabata "this year," which was rather rhapsodic, we had finished writing our wishes on the cards and afterward Asahina had invited me to travel back in time with her to this moment. I was then reunited with the adult version of Asahina and directed to head to East Middle School at night. That was where I ran into a seventh-grade Haruhi plastered to the school gate and found myself drawing a message to outer space with lime on the school grounds.

After that, the high school Asahina, Asahina (Small), lost her TPDD, which was something like a time machine, so I took her to Nagato's apartment, where the two of us were put to sleep for three years and returned to our original time...

"Which means that..."

This was simpler than subtraction. I just had to remember what I could. Yeah, I finally had what I needed. The circumstances necessary for returning this crazy world to the way it had been.

I mean, right?

My legs weren't shaking because of fear. That's right. They were shaking with excitement.

Three years ago. Tanabata. East Middle. Pictograph. John Smith.

I went through the various factors in my mind before finally reaching a conclusion. A simple and clear conclusion. I'll say it again.

"Which means that..."

They would be **here**.

The enthralling and voluptuous adult Asahina—Asahina (Big)—and Yuki Nagato in standby mode.

There were two people in this time who could give me help.

I instantly dropped the newspaper and shot out of the convenience store. Then I began to think as I ran.

During my first trip to three years ago—now—Asahina had said that it was around nine PM when I woke up on the bench in the park in front of Kouyouen Station. I could make it there in thirty minutes if I ran. The problem would be if the changes to the world had affected this time as well. If that was the case, I couldn't possibly be here. I absolutely had to make contact with Asahina (Big) or Nagato in her apartment. Or both, possibly. Which meant there were two places I needed to go, but for now I should head there.

I could go find Nagato in her apartment later. But I'd only be able to find Asahina (Big) at that time and place.

The grown-up Asahina, who was dressed like a teacher. The future Asahina, who gave me the Snow White hint before leaving immediately afterward. I could still remember, as though it had happened yesterday, her poking the cheek of the sleeping beauty Asahina (Small) with a smile on her face.

That Asahina would be able to recognize me. I'm sure of it.

* * *

The park wasn't very far from the station, yet there were barely any people passing by. Maybe because it was night. That would be why it's such a convenient place for suspicious people who pop out after dark. Like a mecca for weirdos—that was how I had felt on that Tanabata. I still feel the same way.

I couldn't make my appearance just yet so I walked along the concrete wall to try to blend into the night. Though the wall itself was only waist-high, there was a wire screen that went up to my head or so. Still, there were trees and bushes all around so it was simple enough to find a place to hide out at night, if not during the day. In fact, I should be more concerned about any people walking behind me giving me funny looks.

I tried to remember the location of the bench I had woken up on as I moved along the wall. I needed to find a suitable spot.

It was almost nine PM.

I was literally peeping through the cracks, I guess. I stuck my head through the bushes to find the scene I had been searching for.

"…That's it, huh?"

It was like watching myself act in a movie, or some kind of dream where I had a third-person perspective.

"Still, this is pretty…"

The bench, under the light from the lamppost, stood out in the darkness as though it were in a spotlight. Even from this far away there was no mistaking it. Both people were wearing North High uniforms. Everything was just as I remembered.

Asahina and I from the past were right there.

That version of me was lying on the bench asleep with his head in Asahina's lap. I'd be lying if I were to say that any dream I'd had in that situation was PG. My head was resting on the most valuable item on the planet. If that didn't lead to a healthy respite, then there was no such thing as sound sleep in this world.

Asahina was peering into my face, which was resting on her thigh, as she blew into my ear and tugged at it. Lucky bastard... wait, that'd be me.

For a moment I was tempted to drag "me" out of there so I could take his place, but I suppressed that urge. "I" hadn't run into a different me at the time. In that case, we'd have a little paradox on our hands if I were to run out there right now—I think? In any case, there wasn't any reason for me to screw up the space-time continuum any further.

I restrained my body's attempt to move against my will as I continued to play a Peeping Tom (or a voyeur, to be more concise). My ability to control myself under these bizarre circumstances spoke well of my character, relatively. I felt like bragging to someone.

And with that in mind I continued my observation when Asahina's lips moved like she was saying something and "I" twitched slightly before sitting up. I couldn't hear their voices from my location but I could still remember. Asahina had just asked if I was awake.

Asahina and "I" appeared to be engaged in small talk, but soon enough Asahina leaned over with the side of her body coming to a rest on "me" with a soft plop—

The bushes behind the bench rustled and that person came out.

I could never forget the long-sleeved white blouse and tight, deep blue miniskirt that made her look like a teacher.

Around the end of May, she had used a letter to set up a meeting and give me the Snow White hint. She also told me about the location of her star-shaped mole. And on this day, Tanabata, she put Asahina (Small) to sleep and instructed me to go to Haruhi before turning and leaving...

The adult version of Asahina.

Her height and body had developed a few more years. An Asahina who came from a future beyond the first Asahina's future. Asahina (Big).

She looked the same as she had then.

This was the verification I needed. It was on that Tanabata day three years ago. Everything was as I remembered.

Asahina (Big) said a few words to "me" before squatting down to poke Asahina (Small) in the cheek and gently pat her back. Then she stood back up and turned to "me" to say something.

—It was her role to guide you to this point. It is my role to guide you from here on.

—Uh…What's going on here…

That was how the conversation went.

"I" stood dumbfounded as Asahina (Big) finished what she needed to say and began walking out of the park without any sign of reluctance. She made her exit from the illuminated spot. For the first time I noticed that she was headed for the park exit on the opposite side from East Middle.

"I" was still spaced out, staring down at the face of the sleeping beauty Asahina (Small) while appearing to be lost in thought. After a few seconds of trying to remember what I had been thinking about, I gave up on jogging through my memory. I couldn't afford to lose sight of Asahina (Big).

I moved from my hiding spot and hurried out of the park. There was no longer any need to hide because "I" never saw me when I was "me" in this situation. The "me" at this time never saw another me from a different time. Never thought that I might. Of course. The past "me" could never have imagined how my space-time would go to hell. I ran off without another look back at the "me" who was so focused on the Asahina behind him that he couldn't think about anything else.

I turned the corner of the park to find her standing about a hundred meters ahead of me. She was walking with her back to me. Her high heels were clicking in a measured beat. She didn't seem to be in a hurry, but unfortunately I was. Everything I'd done to make it to this point would be for nothing if I lost sight of her now.

I began to run again. As I closed in, I could see her beautiful arms and legs and wavy medium-length hair almost shine under the faint light in the night. From behind, I could tell that it was definitely her.

I quickly caught up and called out.

"Asahina!"

She froze. The soft tapping from her heels stopped. Her soft chestnut hair blew across her back. It was like everything was moving in slow motion. She turned around gradually.

I tried to predict what she would say.

—Why? Didn't we just part ways?

—You chased after me...or I suppose not.

—Hmm? What happened to the other me?

The answer was none of the above.

"Good evening, Kyon."

She greeted me with a captivating smile on a face just as beautiful as I remembered.

"I haven't seen *you* in a while."

The adult version of Asahina winked as she said that. It's been a little over five months since I've seen this smile.

Asahina (Big) had a look on her face like a child breathing a sigh of relief.

"Still, I'm glad that we were able to meet here. I was a little worried. After all, I couldn't be sure I hadn't made any mistakes. I still screw up all the time," Asahina said as she stuck out her tongue adorably.

That gesture was lovely enough to make me melt, but I'd lose everything if I gave in now.

This Asahina knew what I needed to do next.

I did my best to hold back my flapping tongue.

"Asahina, you knew that I'd be back…You knew that I would return to this place at this time, didn't you?"

"Yes," Asahina said. "Since it was established information."

"You were the one who arranged for the small Asahina and me to go back three years in time on that Tanabata…in other words, to this time."

"Yes. It was absolutely necessary. Otherwise you wouldn't be here now, right?"

If I hadn't drawn the geoglyph on the East Middle school grounds, I would never have named myself to the seventh-grade Haruhi as John Smith. Naturally, the freshman Haruhi at Kouyouen Academy wouldn't have recognized the name. Which meant that I wouldn't have been able to find a link, since there had been absolutely nothing else to connect that Haruhi to me. And as a result, the five of us wouldn't have assembled in the clubroom and the escape program wouldn't have done its thing.

This was when a question came up. The other John Smith…it couldn't be.

"It was you. Kyon. The present you."

Asahina (Big) smiled at me like a white rose.

"It's rather tiring to talk while standing, so why don't we go find a place to sit down? We still have time."

Her smile and words held enough power to dispel the shroud of unease and confusion surrounding me.

If Asahina (Big) was here, the future still existed. And it wasn't a future that had gone out of whack on the eighteenth. It was the future where I and the Haruhi and Asahina I knew belonged.

It was going to be okay.

I now felt confident enough to calm down. She continued to bolster that confidence.

"It is my role to guide you from here on. However, after that, you'll be on your own. I can only follow your lead."

And then she shut one eye. A perfect wink that almost sent me to my knees.

We went back to the park and sat down on the bench where Asahina (Small) and "I" had been sitting. Before we sat down, Asahina (Big) gently caressed the bench as though it were an ancestral relic, which left me feeling solemn as I sat down. The bench was still warm. The warmth from the Asahina and me who had traveled back three years in time five months ago.

I immediately broke the silence.

"What's up with the flow of time? I can understand how this Tanabata is connected to the time I just came from. Or else I wouldn't have made it here. In that case, Asahina...wouldn't that mean your future was also connected to that altered time?"

"I can't tell you any details."

Figured as much. It was probably classified information.

"No."

Asahina (Big) shook her head.

"I wouldn't be able to explain it in a way you could understand. Our space-time continuum theory is based on a unique concept. I wouldn't be able to convey the idea through words. Do you remember when I first confessed my true identity?"

I recalled the shocking revelation by the cherry blossom trees along the river when Asahina, who I'd thought to be an adorable upperclassman, declared that she was from the future.

"My explanation didn't make much sense, did it? That's the best I can do. I'll only confuse you if I try."

Asahina (Big) tapped herself on the side of her head with her fist as she winked. Every little gesture she made felt so sensual.

"A concept cannot be explained through words when the necessary terms don't exist yet. Do you understand that?"

How could I? My head was spinning as Asahina spoke to me as if she were trying to teach a preschooler differential equations.

"Uh-huh. Still, you'll understand soon enough. I'm sure. That's all I can say for now."

I'll understand soon enough—pretty sure that someone else said something similar to that before summer vacation. Right, Nagato said something along those lines...Wait.

A flash of electricity ran through my synapses as I replied.

"Before summer vacation...the stuff Nagato mentioned during the incident with the cave cricket...About how computers in the future weren't anything like the ones now, was that..."

"Ah, that's a sharp observation. You still remember? That's right. The system in our time that serves as a computer or network does not rely on any material substance. It exists within our minds in an abstract form. The TPDD is also that way."

The thing she lost that was supposed to be impossible to lose.

"Is that a time machine?"

"Time Plane Destroid Device."

Shouldn't that be classified information?

"Yes, it was for me back then. The restrictions on me are slightly more relaxed now. Since I've worked very hard to come this far."

Asahina puffed up her chest, which almost sent a button flying off her blouse. Her physically impossible body proportions were impressed on me in a beguiling fashion, but unfortunately my mind was unable to find optical refuge in that sight.

I asked, "What was the cause? I understand the future I was in had been changed. But when did it change?"

"It would be better to ask the Nagato in this time period for the details. But I can tell you one thing. Your time plane was altered three years from 'now' on the morning of December eighteenth."

That would be two days ago for me. Alteration to the time plane, huh? Which meant that…I tried to remember the two interpretations Koizumi had come up with. I guess that the one that didn't involve parallel worlds was correct.

"Yes. STC data…um, the entire world was changed overnight. Only your memories remained untouched. It was an incredible timequake that could be observed from the distant future."

It wasn't that I had no interest in technical terms like "STC" or "timequake," but I didn't have time to waste on trivial matters. There were other more pressing questions to deal with.

"If you were waiting here for me, Asahina, does that mean you'll also be dealing with the disaster that has befallen my future?"

"I cannot deal with it alone," she replied with a glum look on her face. "We need Nagato's help. And you also have to be with us."

"Who's responsible for this? I'm guessing it was Haruhi."

"It wasn't."

Asahina's smile faded as she continued in a soft voice.

"It wasn't Suzumiya. Someone else was responsible for this."

"A new character? Some freak who came crashing in from another dimension—"

"No."

Asahina almost sounded wistful as she interrupted me.

"It was someone you know very well."

Asahina (Big) checked her watch and noted that we still had some time, so we began reminiscing about the SOS Brigade. In my case, less than a year had passed, but I got the impression that it had been many years for her. Starting with Haruhi carrying her away to the clubroom, forcing her to dress up like a bunny girl, the wishes on Tanabata, the murder show on the island, wearing a summer kimono for the Bon Dance, doing summer homework with everyone else in the brigade, filming the movie…Asahina (Big) began talking more slowly as she reached the parts that were still fresh in my mind.

I was waiting for her to accidentally reveal a story that would be in my future, but this Asahina was cautious. Our conversation was limited to minor chitchat.

"It was quite an ordeal, but they were all fond memories."

And after that final observation, Asahina shut her mouth. She continued to stare at me in silence.

I was wondering if I should make an appropriate comment when something soft and warm landed on my shoulder. It was the head belonging to Asahina (Big), but I couldn't even imagine what this action was supposed to mean, as the body pressing against mine was certainly worth its weight in gold and my mind was a total mess because the sweet fragrance and sensation were incapacitating me. I could feel the soft warmth of her body through the cloth of her shirt. What was she trying to say? Was she trying to sense something from my body? Asahina (Big) had her eyes shut as she leaned her face into my shoulder and her lips moved without making a sound. She was saying something inaudibly. I wonder what.

No way, I thought in a daze. Don't tell me that this Asahina is going to fall asleep and then another Asahina will show up from behind to confuse me with more weird talk. And then I'd just keep on running into Asahinas from different times forever—no, I was starting to think in circles like laundry spinning round in a dryer. Hey, what am I doing here? Somebody tell me.

Asahina (Big) was nestled against me for about a minute.

"Hehe."

She smiled as though reading my thoughts.

"It's almost time. Let's go."

She stood up as though nothing had happened. Sadly, I had to return to my senses. That's right. I needed to go. Uh, where are we going?

To my second destination.

Asahina's wristwatch told us that it was a little before ten PM. That would be after "I" had finished defacing East Middle's school grounds with the seventh-grade Haruhi and dragged a weeping Asahina to Nagato's apartment. Around the time when "I" had my time frozen.

I needed to ask Nagato for help again.

"But first," Asahina said, as a heartwarming smile hit her face like a starry sky, "there's something else you must do, right?"

We left the park and soon found ourselves inside a residential area.

I followed Asahina's cue and headed down an alley.

I could see a small shadow marching at the end of the dark street. The thin arms and legs that extended from her T-shirt and shorts swished around with her somewhat long hair as she walked.

"Hey!"

I could see the short shadow in T-shirt and shorts turn around in the distance. Once I was sure that she had seen me, I cupped my hands like a megaphone and shouted. Loud enough to blow off some steam.

"Cheers to saving the world by overloading it with fun with John Smith!"

The seventh-grade girl appeared to be staring my way before turning in a huff and stomping off.

She must have thought that there wasn't any hurry, since she'd be able to find me at North High later on, which was why she walked away without any hesitation. As I watched her somewhat long, black hair depart, I added in a soft voice, "Please remember the name John Smith, Haruhi…"

I prayed from the bottom of my heart to a twelve-year-old Haruhi, a Haruhi who would continue to run wild at East Middle.

Please don't forget. That I was here.

I could probably have made my way to the fancy apartment blindfolded, since I'd practically memorized the path by now. Asahina (Big) was walking behind me to the side in a subdued manner as I looked up at the brand-new building I had just visited around twenty hours ago. Asahina (Big) seemed to be hiding her nice body behind me as though she was expecting someone to show up.

"…Kyon, I have a favor to ask."

I had no reason to turn down her pleas. I wasn't cruel enough to ignore a request from any Asahina from any time.

"Sorry. I'm still uncomfortable around Nagato…"

Right, Asahina (Small) was acting the same way when we came here last time. Haruhi aside, Koizumi was the only one who was able to conduct himself in a neutral manner around aliens and time travelers.

"Well, I can understand how you feel."

I tried to sound considerate as I entered 708 into the keypad and pressed the button to ring the bell.

After a few seconds I heard a click over the intercom.

I was greeted by a duet of wordless and soundless.

"Nagato, it's me."

—Silence.

"Sorry, it's a little hard to explain, but I'm back from the future. Asahina's also here. The grown-up one. Uh, yeah, her time-divergent variant, was it?"

—Silence.

"I need your help. Or actually, the future you sent me here."

—Silence.

"Asahina and I should be up there. Asleep in your guest room with our time frozen…"

There was a click as the entrance was unlocked.

"Come in."

The sound of Nagato's voice through the intercom was comforting to hear. It was her usual flat voice, cool and soft. There seemed to be a subtle twinge of wonder and surprise mixed in, but it was probably just my imagination. The sky was the limit once Nagato took over. She'll be able to do something about this situation. Or I'm screwed.

Asahina's fingers were hooked in my belt, and she appeared as nervous as if she were walking on a fence in high heels. The elevator doors opened and inhaled us before heading up…

To the now-familiar room 708.

There was a doorbell, but I wasn't in the mood. I knocked on the door without a word. I couldn't sense anybody on the other side, but the metal door soon opened.

"…"

A small spectacled face peeked through the crack in the door. She stared at me and swiveled her head to focus on Asahina (Big) before returning her gaze to me.

"…"

The empty reaction with no expression on her face or words

spoken almost made me want to beg her to say something, any-thing at all. This was vintage Nagato. The Nagato from when we first met. The one who'd been aloof back during spring. The one "I" had asked for help "three years ago."

"May we come in?"

After a moment of silent thought, Nagato's chin dipped about a millimeter and she retreated into the room. I'm guessing that's a yes. I turned to the tense beauty behind me.

"Let's go, Asahina."

"Yes…You're right. It should be fine."

She sounded like she was trying to reassure herself.

Still, how many times have I entered this room? Four times in total, but only twice if I counted chronologically? My sense of time was a train wreck. I was surprised that my biological clock hadn't gone haywire yet. My body should have collapsed after jumping from winter to summer and going back in time three years twice, but everything was functioning normally for now. In fact, I was tempted to say that my mind had never been clearer. Because I'd gotten used to it? Maybe after going through all these surreal experiences, I'd managed to fry the nerves that recognized what was normal.

Nagato's room was just as empty as I'd remembered, without any signs of being inhabited. Just the way it'd been "three years ago." Just the way it'd been when I first visited back in May.

I was able to relax because this Yuki Nagato was the one I knew. No expression on her face, no emotion shown. A completely infallible alien who never acted confused.

I took off my shoes and made my way through the narrow hall-way to reach the living room. Nagato was waiting there. Standing all alone with her eyes fixed on Asahina and me in silence. Even if she was surprised, I wouldn't be able to tell by looking at her face. It was possible that this Nagato saw me visit from the future on a regular basis, though I doubt that I'll be traveling through time to this day that many times.

"We shouldn't need to introduce ourselves, right?"

Nagato had yet to sit down, so Asahina and I also remained standing.

"This is the adult version of Asahina. You've met her before," I said before remembering that it wouldn't happen for another three years. "I mean, you're going to meet her. Yeah, she's definitely Asahina, so it's fine."

Nagato stared at Asahina (Big) the way you'd stare at a Math IIB problem on an entrance exam and let her eyes drift toward the guest room before returning to stare at the well-endowed body hiding behind me.

"Understood."

She nodded without a single hair's moving.

As I followed Nagato's gaze, I couldn't help finding myself drawn to that special partitioned-off room next to the living room.

"Can I open it?"

I pointed to the guest room and Nagato shook her head.

"It will not open. The room structure has been frozen along with time."

That brought on a mixture of regret and relief.

I felt a warm breath on the back of my neck. Asahina (Big) had let out a soft sigh. She apparently felt the same way I did. I wondered how Asahina (Big) would feel if she saw herself sleeping next to me. I was tempted to ask, but I needed to explain the situation first.

"Nagato, sorry about bothering you again, but could you at least hear me out?"

How much had the "me" in the adjacent room told her? The history of the SOS Brigade up till the Tanabata fiasco. Then I simply needed to pick up from there. A tale spanning half a year or so, which started from a spring of melancholy, led to a parade of activities for alleviating Haruhi's boredom, and concluded with the film shooting that forced me to sigh. Yes, you were also there, Nagato. You were a big help at times, though you also gave me a few scares. Until two days ago. For some reason, none of that had ever happened, which was why I came here. With the help of a Nagato-made emergency escape program.

It would have taken a few hours to explain if I went into detail, so I gave her the same digest I'd given Haruhi. Skipped over the nitty-gritty stuff and gave her the general storyline. That should be enough for her.

"...And so I managed to make it back here, thanks to you."

The proof of the pudding is in the eating, so I took the bookmark from my pocket. I felt like I was handing a talisman to a ghost as I showed it to Nagato.

"..."

Nagato took the bookmark in her fingertips and ignored the illustration of a flower as her eyes fell on the writing on the back. Her scrutiny was what I'd expect from an archaeologist who had just dug up an LCD TV from a Cretaceous stratum. I had no idea how long she was going to stare at the thing, so I interrupted her inspection with a question.

"What should we do?"

"I-I believe that we should normalize this abnormal space-time."

Asahina (Big)'s voice sounded as nervous as if she were confessing her love to the man of her dreams. Asahina had a tendency to act like a nervous wreck around Nagato, and it seemed as though that hadn't changed years later. That was the impression I got.

"Nagato...We need your help. You are the only one who can restore this altered time plane. Please..."

Asahina (Big) had her hands clasped together and eyes shut tight, as though she were praying at a shrine. I'll join in the prayer to the great goddess Nagato. Return the world to one where Asahina would make tea for us in the clubroom, which I would savor while playing a board game with Koizumi, and you would be sitting as still as a statue next to us while reading a book until Haruhi came flying through the door. That was my wish.

"…"

Nagato looked up from the bookmark to stare at empty space with earnest eyes. I could understand why Asahina was so nervous. We had no chance of winning if Nagato disagreed. Was there anybody in this world who could stand against Nagato? Maybe Haruhi.

We couldn't hear any outside noise in the soundproofed apartment room. It was as quiet as if time had stopped. Nagato's eyes met mine. A gesture of acceptance. The one where her chin moved a few millimeters.

"Confirming," Nagato said, shutting her eyes before I could ask what she was confirming.

"…"

Her eyes immediately reopened as she turned eyes the color of night toward me.

"Unable to synchronize."

Another short phrase as she stared at me. Her face looked slightly different, and it probably wasn't an optical illusion. This face was the product of everything that had happened since spring and over the summer. Koizumi had also noticed. The culmination of all the minuscule changes to Nagato's expression since we first met. However, this wasn't how Nagato had been by winter.

Her thin lips parted slightly.

"I am unable to access that time continuum. The system is equipped with a protection that selectively rejects my requests."

I didn't understand what that meant, but I was pretty worried. Hey, hold on a sec. Don't tell me that there's nothing you can do.

Nagato paid no heed to my fears.

"But the situation has been understood. Restoration is possible."

She slowly traced the words on the bookmark with her finger. And then she began to explain in a voice that sounded like newly accumulating snowfall.

"The party responsible for the space-time alteration manipulated Haruhi Suzumiya's data creation ability to partially transform the data composition of the world."

The soft voice I was used to hearing. It soothed my heart the way a music-box tune soothed me as a baby.

"As a result, Haruhi Suzumiya was left powerless after the alteration. She no longer has the power to create data. The Data Overmind does not exist in that space-time."

I didn't get it, but that sounded pretty ominous, since the past had been rewritten for every person around Haruhi, except me. An all-girls school had been turned into a coed one, a number of North High students had been shifted to that school, all related parties had had their memories altered accordingly, the members of the Agency, Nagato the alien, and Asahina the time traveler were all living different lives, Asakura was back in action, and Haruhi had been erased from the memories of the students at North High. Asakura had been added in and Haruhi taken out. Even Nagato's boss was gone.

What a mess.

"The power stolen from Haruhi Suzumiya allowed the perpetrator to modify three hundred sixty-five days' worth of memory data."

So the period from December of last year—going by my original time—to December seventeenth of the current year had been modified. The Tanabata three years earlier—which would be today—had been left untouched. Now there's a lifesaver. I only made it this far because Haruhi still remembered what had happened on Tanabata. Still, who was the fool who did something as stupid as something Haruhi would do?

Nagato was still staring at me.

"Restoring the world will require traveling to December eighteenth three years from now and running the repair program immediately after the perpetrator alters space-time."

So you're going to travel through time with us? Since you're the one who's doing the repairing?

"I cannot go."

Why not?

"Because," Nagato answered as she pointed to the guest room, "I cannot leave them."

Her explanation was that she couldn't leave this space-time while keeping time frozen for Asahina and me, sleeping in the next room. Nagato continued in an announcer-like tone.

"Emergency mode."

"So what are we supposed to do?" I asked, feeling a little anxious.

"Mixing."

As usual, she failed to make any sense.

Nagato slowly removed her glasses and held them in both hands. The glasses then levitated above her palms, as though they were being held up by invisible strings. If this had been a normal person, there probably would have been invisible strings involved, but I shouldn't have to tell you that Nagato doesn't do normal.

Squish.

The lenses and frame twisted into a weird whirlpool for a moment before the glasses transformed into something completely different. A shape I recognized. One that most people would prefer to avoid. A tool that humans instinctively feared.

I hesitantly offered my view.

"It looks like a giant syringe..."

"Yes."

It was filled with a colorless, transparent liquid. What are we supposed to do with that, and to whom?

"Inject the repair program into the perpetrator."

I glanced at the sharp needle protruding from the syringe before reflexively looking away.

"Uh...Isn't there a more peaceful way to go about this? I'm sorry to say that I'm not licensed for any of that stuff. It might get ugly if I hit the wrong spot."

Nagato turned to the syringe clenched in her hands with eyes the color of a powered-off LCD screen.

"I see."

Her hands opened to reveal the syringe swirling into something else. I recognized the shape and gulped.

"That's a dangerous item you've got there..."

It was a handgun this time. However, the barrel was especially small and appeared to be stainless steel.

Nagato offered the shiny metallic model-gun-like pistol to me.

"Probability of success remains high through clothing, but a direct discharge to the skin is preferred."

"What about bullets? Don't tell me you're using live ammunition."

Going by the appearance of the fake-looking gun, they were either aluminum or plastic.

"Needle gun. The program has been applied to the tip of the needle."

Mentally more acceptable than a giant syringe. I took the gun and was surprised by how light it was.

"By the way…"

I finally asked the question I'd been avoiding.

"Who's responsible? Who changed the world? Who besides Haruhi could it be? Tell me."

I could hear Asahina (Big) sigh softly.

Nagato's lips parted as she nonchalantly told me **that person**'s name.

CHAPTER 5

"..."

I was struggling to find an appropriate response when Nagato turned to Asahina (Big).

"Transmitting target space-time coordinates."

"Oh, yes."

Asahina (Big) stuck out her hand as though she were a large, loyal dog.

"Go ahead..."

Nagato's finger lightly touched the back of Asahina (Big)'s hand before it was slowly retracted.... That was it? However, that appeared to be enough for Asahina (Big).

"I understand, Nagato. We simply have to go to that point and repair 'her.' It shouldn't be difficult. Since that version of 'her' won't have any power to speak of..."

The time traveler clenched her fists in determination as she spoke to the alien.

"Wait."

The removal of Nagato's glasses had left her face bare, though still unruffled.

"As of now, you would be caught in the space-time transformation. Applying countermeasure."

She extended her arm without a sound.

"Your hand."

What? You want to shake hands or something? I obediently stuck my right hand out and Nagato grabbed my wrist with her cold fingers, giving me a scare.

"…"

Nagato's somber face turned to my arm.

"Whoa!"

I let out a cry without meaning to. But you couldn't blame me for reacting that way. Nagato had leaned over to place her lips on my wrist and bite down, even. The way I'd seen her bite Asahina multiple times while shooting the movie.

It was a soft bite without any animosity, like the ones Shamisen gave me when we were playing around. But the sensation of her cuspids on my skin was a little itchy. The penetration certainly didn't hurt, but Nagato might have had something in her saliva to numb the pain, the way a mosquito did.

Nagato's teeth remained planted in my wrist for five or ten seconds before she slowly looked up.

"An operational counter-data screen and protective field have been applied to the surface of your body."

Nagato didn't turn red or blush. Asahina (Big) was the one covering her mouth with both hands in surprise. I looked at my wrist, which still felt slightly numb. There were two tiny holes, as if I'd been attacked by a vampire, that were closing up before my eyes. So Nagato's special nanomachines had been injected into my body, like what had happened to Asahina during the film shoot.

"And you."

Asahina timidly extended a trembling arm in response to Naga-to's solicitation.

"…It's been a long time since I've experienced this. Sorry about all the trouble I caused back then…"

"This is my first time."

"Ah. Th-that's right. I wasn't thinking…"

The time traveler kept her eyes shut tight as the alien kissed her wrist and injected the suspect nanomachines for what felt like a shorter period of time than I had endured, before coughing when it was all done.

"Then let's go, Kyon. Time for the main event."

The introduction was way too long then, if that's the case. Still, I've done my best to narrate the chain of events. Though I never want to do it again.

"Thanks."

I voiced my gratitude to the composed owner of the room. Nagato, silence incarnate, didn't reply. No sign of emotion on her face. Yet for some reason Nagato, standing tall and erect, looked lonely somehow. Was that how it was? My guess had been right?

"See you later, Nagato. Sit tight in the literary club until Haruhi and I show up."

Like a china doll come to life, the alien-made organic life-form nodded her head in a mechanical motion.

"I will be waiting."

Her soft voice left a funny feeling in my chest. But I didn't get a chance to identify this hazy-like-cigarette-smoke feeling because Asahina (Big) cut in.

"We don't want you to get temporal sickness."

She poked me in the shoulder.

"Close your eyes."

I did as she said. I could sense Asahina (Big) standing in front of me. She grabbed my wrists.

"Kyon..."

Her soft, whispering voice was sweet music to my ears. Shouldn't she throw in a kiss as an extra bonus?

"Here I go."

Go right on ahead. As many intense ones as you'd like, and the moment that thought was out of my head—

I was hit by a dramatic wave of dizziness. Good thing my eyes were closed. I probably would have blacked out if they'd been open. This was like riding a roller coaster without wearing seat belts. I couldn't tell if I was feeling light-headed or if blood was rushing into my head. I felt like I was floating in zero gravity as my head spun around despite the fact that my eyes were closed. I hadn't lost consciousness only because of the warm sensation of Asahina (Big)'s skin against my arm.

How many minutes passed? How many hours? I was losing my sense of time and space. I've reached my limit. I'm about to throw up, Asahina...

I fumbled around for something to serve as a substitute for a sick bag.

"Okay...we're here."

The sensation of standing on solid ground had returned. I could feel the cold ground through my shoes. And at the same time my entire body was once again at the mercy of the Earth's gravity. My urge to puke was gone like it had never existed.

"You can open your eyes now. That's a relief. We've arrived at the place and...time Nagato indicated."

I looked up. I could see winter constellations sparkling in the night sky. The air was cleaner, which meant that the stars were more lucid than they were in summer. I turned my head to spot the top of the North High school building sticking out above the houses.

I looked around to check our current position. It was dark in the dead of night, but I knew for sure where we were. I'd been here a few hours ago. I could even remember Haruhi with a ponytail and Koizumi in gym clothes standing here.

By coincidence, we were at the spot where Haruhi and Koizumi had changed clothes. A coincidence—I think.

So when was this?

Asahina (Big) checked her watch and told me.

"Four eighteen AM on December eighteenth. The world will change in five minutes."

Going from the twentieth, when I pressed the Enter key to be sent three years back in time, the eighteenth would be two days earlier. On that day I had woken up and gone to school like always, without a care, before finding myself in a panic because North High had completely changed. Haruhi no longer existed, Asakura had returned, Asahina didn't know me, and Nagato was an ordinary human.

This was when it all began. I was currently at the moment when it would begin. In that case, I had a chance to prevent it from happening. That was why I was here right now.

I was feeling all serious and determined when...

"Oh, my shoes. I forgot them," Asahina (Big) murmured in a flustered voice.

Since we had come directly from the living room without putting our shoes on. That's Asahina for you. Years later, and she was still a klutz.

"I wonder if Nagato will hold on to them for me."

I had to smile upon hearing her anxious voice. You shouldn't need to worry. She held on to that card for three years, so she probably wouldn't throw away shoes. I'll check her shoe stand the next time I visit her room...

As soon as I finished with that line of thought, my body shook as if I'd been hit by lightning.

Jumping barefoot from summer to the middle of winter had left me feeling really cold. I was about to put on the jacket I was carrying when I noticed that Asahina (Big) was hugging herself against the cold. Well, she was probably freezing, since she was wearing a blouse and miniskirt in this temperature.

"Here, take this."

I laid my jacket on her trembling shoulder. The chivalrous act helped to boost my ego.

"Th-thank you. Sorry about that."

It's no big deal. I was able to make it back here because you were waiting for me three years ago. From that perspective, I'd be willing to give up every article of clothing I'm wearing.

Asahina (Big) giggled as she presented me with a sexy and cute smile that was dazzling enough to send half of the human race to its knees, before getting a serious look on her face.

"It's almost time."

It was probably a good thing that we had forgotten our shoes. We needed to walk without making any sound. Still, Asahina and I kept our breathing to a minimum as we crept toward the entrance to North High. We stopped at the corner and glanced around the dark street surreptitiously, as though we were stalking prey.

There weren't many streetlights around, but there happened to be one right in front of the gate. It illuminated that particular area like a diffused spotlight. There wasn't much light, but it was bright enough for us to tell that someone was standing there.

"There she is…"

A warm hand fell upon my shoulder. Asahina (Big) was nervously breathing softly into my ear, which normally would have left me entranced, but in this situation I had to banish those thoughts from my mind.

The perpetrator emerged from the night as **she** walked near the streetlight.

A North High uniform. The person whom Nagato had named. **She** was the one who had changed our world and scattered the members of the SOS Brigade while turning them into normal people. The one who had left my memories intact while changing history for every other person.

She was about to commit that very act.

I couldn't jump out yet. Nagato had advised us to watch everything happen. We had to let **her** change the world before we could fire the repair program. The reasoning was that my activation of the escape program would be erased from history otherwise, which really didn't make any sense at all, but Nagato and Asahina (Big) seemed pretty sure of themselves. Those two probably know what they're talking about when it comes to the flow of time. I sure don't. I have no chance of understanding, so I should simply follow the instructions of people who do. Nagato wouldn't lie to me. She always stood on our side with a serious look on her face…

I clenched the needle gun Nagato had given me and waited for time to pass.

She walked quietly toward the North High entrance before coming to a stop as **she** looked up at the cheap building, shrouded in darkness.

Her sailor uniform skirt was fluttering in the wind.

She hadn't noticed us watching. Probably thanks to the nano-machines Nagato had injected into us. The screen-and-protective-shield thing.

She suddenly raised one arm, as though **she** were trying to grab the air. A rather unnatural motion that made me wonder if someone else was controlling **her**, but I already knew that wasn't the case.

"Amazing…" Asahina murmured in admiration. "It's a powerful timequake. I never would have imagined that she had so much power…It's hard to believe, even as I'm witnessing it happen."

Witness it happen? I haven't seen a single thing change. It was still nighttime. But Asahina (Big) was somehow able to sense the history of this world being altered. I mean, she is from the future. She should know a trick or two.

Asahina (Big) was leaning against me. Originally we would have been caught up in the transformation to the world, but Nagato's bite had solved that problem. Nagato and Asahina (Big). I couldn't do anything without the two of them. I made the right move. My next move should resolve the current mess. Can't afford to screw up this last bit.

I held my breath and watched as **she** lowered her arm and abruptly turned in our direction. For a second I thought that **she** had noticed us hiding here, but **she** was apparently just looking around.

"Don't worry. We haven't been discovered. She was just reborn. The timequake…alteration to the world has ended. Kyon, it's our turn now."

Asahina (Big)'s firm and serious tone served as a signal.

I moved out of the darkness and headed for the school gate. No need to rush, since **she** wasn't going to run away. As expected, **she** didn't budge from her spot before the school gate upon noticing me stepping into the light. Only her expression changed. The look of surprise left me feeling somewhat melancholy.

"Yo."

I walked over as though I had just run into an old friend.

"It's me. We meet again."

I'd more or less figured it out from the tone of Asahina (Big)'s voice. Who besides Haruhi out of the people I knew could be capable of such a thing? Just think. After the eighteenth the members of the SOS Brigade all lost their secret identities. However, their personalities didn't change. Only one person acted and behaved differently from before.

The small figure wearing a North High uniform stood in the darkness. That person was glancing around, wondering why **she** was here, like a sleepwalker who had just woken up—

"Nagato."

I opened my mouth.

"So it was you."

She was wearing glasses. This was the other Nagato. The Yuki Nagato after the eighteenth, who was nothing more than the sole member of the literary club. No longer an alien. Just a shy bookworm.

The spectacled Nagato looked at me in surprise, like she didn't understand what was going on.

"…Why are you here?" she asked.

"What about you? Do you know why you're here?"

"…A walk."

Nagato spoke in a subdued voice. The girl's eyes widened as she looked at me, and her glasses were reflecting the streetlight's glare. That was when I thought.

No. That's not it, Nagato.

She'd been tired. After enduring Haruhi's sporadic ideas, protecting me from harm, engaging in secret activities the rest of us didn't know about—she'd built up a lot of fatigue after everything she'd been through.

The Nagato from three years ago had told me when I was in her room a moment ago.

"The accumulation of erroneous data in my memory space led to the bug that triggered abnormal behavior. This has been determined to be an inevitable event. I will invariably reconstruct the world on December eighteenth in three years."

Then she continued in a flat voice.

"There is no countermeasure. For I do not know the cause of the error."

I knew.

The trigger that led to Nagato's behaving in a way she couldn't understand. What led to the accumulation of erroneous data.

It was a typical plotline. Whether it was in an artificial intelligence, supposedly only able to act according to a program, or in a robot missing the necessary circuit, that element would develop over the course of time. You wouldn't understand. But I do. And Haruhi also would.

I took my time observing Nagato's confused face. The inconspicuous literary club member looked uncomfortable as she stood still. I spoke to the ephemeral girl in my mind.

—You see, Nagato. You've learned to feel.

The fact that you were designed to not feel any emotion only made it worse. You probably wanted to scream and rage and tell a certain person off. Well, that's what Nagato should have done, even if she didn't feel that way. I should have told her to do that. The responsibility was mine. I'd become too dependent after getting used to letting Nagato handle everything. I was a fool who never bothered to think beyond how Nagato would save the day. Stupider than Haruhi, even. I didn't have the right to criticize anybody else.

And as a result, Nagato—this girl—snapped and tried to change the world.

A bug? Error?

Get out. It wasn't anything like that.

This was Nagato's wish. Nagato wished for such a normal world.

She changed everyone, including herself, leaving only my memory intact.

The answer to the question that had troubled me for the past few days was finally clear.

—Why was I the only one left unchanged?

The answer was simple. She'd given me the right to make a choice.

A scenario where I was supposed to choose between the changed world and the original world.

"Damn it."

What kind of choice is that?

Sure, we could still re-form the SOS Brigade. Haruhi and Koizumi were at a different school, but that wasn't much of an obstacle. We could operate outside of school. An obscure club that hung out at the usual café. Haruhi would still come up with crazy ideas while Koizumi smiled, as always. Asahina would be all confused while I grimaced and stared into the distance. And Nagato would be there in her unstable emotional state while reading a book in silence. However—

That wouldn't be the SOS Brigade I knew. Nagato wouldn't be an alien, Asahina wouldn't be a time traveler, Koizumi would be an ordinary person, and Haruhi would have no special powers at all. We'd just be a normal group of ordinary buddies.

Was I okay with that? Would it be better that way?

What did I think? How did I feel about the ridiculous incidents and events Haruhi had created?

Sick of this.

Give me a break.

Waste of time.

Not putting up with any more of this.

"…"

I felt a sharp pain in my heart.

An ordinary person who was unwillingly dragged into mess after mess. A high school student who would complain but still struggle to meet Haruhi's unreasonable demands. That was supposed to be my role.

So then, me. Yes, you. I'm talking to myself. This is an important question, so listen carefully before answering. You aren't allowed to plead the Fifth. A simple yes or no works. Okay? Here comes the question.

—Was that abnormal school lifestyle fun for you?

Answer, me. Think. Well? Tell me how you feel about it. Go on. I've been dragged around by Haruhi, attacked by an alien, given odd explanations by a time traveler, given more odd explanations by an esper, trapped in closed space while giants rampaged around, cats talked, and I somehow traveled through time, all while following the strict rule of having to hide everything from Haruhi so the SOS Brigade chief could search for the supernatural while blissfully oblivious. Not very consistent when she doesn't realize what she's doing.

Wasn't that all fun?

Sick of this. Give me a break. Waste of time. Not putting up with any more of this. Oh, really? In that case, this was how you felt.

—It was a total drag.

Right? That would be the obvious conclusion. If you were truly annoyed by Haruhi to the point where everything about her pissed you off, you wouldn't be able to enjoy yourself. You can't deny it. Clear as day.

However, you had fun. The original world was more interesting.

How do I know this?
Allow me to explain.

—Didn't you press the Enter key?

The emergency escape program. The corrective utility.
Ready?
You answered that question with a yes.
Right?
The mighty Nagato had calmed the world down for you, yet you rejected that. You accepted the stupid hodgepodge world where you met Haruhi Suzumiya in April. You wanted to return to a world that was practically delusional—where an alien, a time traveler, and an esper boy were all roaming the hallways of the same school.

Why is that, eh? Weren't you complaining all the time? Lamenting about how miserable you were?

In that case, you should have ignored the escape program, right? That way you would have gotten to know Haruhi, Asahina, Koizumi, and Nagato as normal high school students and enjoyed a fairly entertaining lifestyle under Haruhi's guidance. Haruhi would have no power, so there wouldn't be any phenomena to wreck everyday life.

Haruhi would be an ordinary human with a big head, Asahina would be a cute damsel in distress who couldn't travel through time, Koizumi would be a typical high school student without any mysterious agency backing him, and Nagato would be a quiet bookworm who wasn't on a weird mission, didn't have any weird powers, didn't have to watch over anybody, and didn't have to protect anybody. That's right. She might have become a person who would usually show no emotion but then suddenly laugh at a silly joke before turning red, the kind of person who would gradually open up over time.

You gave up on that alternative life.

Why did you do that?

I'll ask again. This is the last time. Give me a straight answer.

Did I think that the trouble-making pseudo-goddess Haruhi and the nightmare she represented were fun? Answer me.

"You bet."

That was my answer.

"It was obviously fun. Don't ask a question when you already know the answer."

If some guy were to answer that he didn't find any of that interesting, he'd be one helluva moron. Thirty times thicker than Haruhi.

I mean, we're talking about aliens, time travelers, and espers here.

One would be more than enough, yet here we have a triple crown of fun. Add in Haruhi and you've got a whole new level of mysterious power at work. How could I not be entertained? I'd beat the crap out of any person who had a beef with that situation.

"There you have it," I said to myself. Or more like snapped at myself.

"That version's better. This world doesn't cut it. Sorry, Nagato. I prefer the Nagato from before over the current you. Besides, you look better without glasses."

That Nagato turned back toward me with a dubious look on her face.

"What are you saying...?"

The Nagato I knew would never say that.

She didn't know anything of the three days that had passed since the morning when I realized something was wrong. Of course. This Nagato was just reborn, so she hadn't spent any time with me yet. She had never looked up in surprise as I flew into the literary club room.

This Nagato only had her fake memory of the library. That was the only memory she had of me at this point.

A while back Haruhi and I had been trapped in gray closed space by ourselves. According to Koizumi, Haruhi had attempted to create a new world.

That's a convenient power. We all find ourselves wishing for a complete redo at some point in our lives and all of us have dreamed about changing reality to suit our individual needs.

However, that would normally be impossible. And probably not a good idea. I had no intention of starting over from scratch. That was why I returned from closed space with Haruhi.

The difference this time was that God, or whatever that strange power was, had shifted from Haruhi to Nagato. Haruhi had done it unconsciously, but Nagato had snapped and consciously changed the world.

"Nagato."

I walked over to the small, petrified figure. Nagato didn't move as she looked up at me.

"My answer is going to be the same every time. Return everything back to the way it was. That includes you. We can do something in the clubroom together again. I'll help you out if you ask. Haruhi's a lot less volatile now. There's no need for you to use this unnecessary power to force a change. Things would have been fine the way they were."

I could see fear in her eyes through her glasses.

"Kyon…"

Asahina was tugging at my shirt sleeve.

"There's no use in talking to this Nagato. After all, she's already been changed. This Nagato has no power at all…she's just a girl…"

I suddenly remembered.

The Haruhi with long hair. The completely ordinary Haruhi who wasn't God or anything else, who called me John, and who sneaked into North High. The one who listened to my SOS Brigade story with shining eyes and said that it sounded fun with a smile.

The Koizumi with a handsome smile who had said that he was attracted to that Haruhi. The overachieving transfer student who made a face as he wore my gym uniform.

The spectacled Nagato who gave me the club application form, invited me to her home, and told me about her false memory of the library trip. A smile, faint as twilight, that I would love to see again.

And I wouldn't be seeing any of them again. To be honest, there were some regrets. But those guys were all fake to begin with. They weren't my Haruhi, Koizumi, Nagato, or Asahina. It was unfortunate that I didn't get a chance to say good-bye, but I was going to take back my Haruhi, Koizumi, Nagato, and Asahina. I've made up my mind.

"Sorry."

I drew the pistol-shaped device. Nagato froze in place, which left me feeling a little guilty. But I couldn't hesitate after coming this far.

"Everything should return to normal soon. We'll be able to go to all kinds of places together again. First would be the Christmas party with hot pot galore. After that we could go to a winter villa or something. You can play the role of detective this time. Are you up for playing a super detective who solves a mystery the second it happens? And then—"

"Kyon! Look out...! Eek!!"

Asahina screamed right as someone crashed into my back. Thud. The impact left me wobbling on my feet and the shadow I cast in the streetlight also shook. The shadow of another person was overlapping mine. What? Who was it?

"I won't allow anyone to hurt Nagato."

I turned my head to look over my shoulder and found a girl's pale face.

Ryoko Asakura.

"Wha…"

I couldn't speak. Something cold was stabbing into my side. A flat object had been thrust deep inside my body. It felt really cold. My anxiety trumped any pain I was feeling. What is this? What the hell? Why is Asakura here?

"Heh heh."

Her smirk was something you'd expect from a mask suddenly bursting into a smile. Asakura moved away in a blur as she pulled out the long and bloody blade that had been stuck in my side.

I found myself spinning like a drill as I tumbled toward the ground after losing my support. I looked in front of me—Nagato was sitting on the ground as though her legs had given out on her. Her quivering lips parted.

"Asakura…"

Asakura waved the bloody combat knife by way of greeting.

"That's right, Nagato. I'm right here. I shall eliminate anything that threatens you. That is why I am here."

Asakura laughed.

"Wasn't that your wish? Right?"

You're lying. Nagato would never wish for this. She would never consider killing a bird because it didn't sing the way she wanted. No. The Nagato who had behaved abnormally. That Nagato had brought back an Asakura who was also abnormal. She was Nagato's shadow…

Asakura's faint silhouette fell across my body. I saw a crescent moon above Asakura's head before it was covered up.

"I'm going to finish you now. You can die. You are tormenting

Nagato. Does it hurt? Of course it does. Savor the pain. It'll be the last thing you feel in this lifetime."

She lifted the gruesome knife. The tip was aimed at my heart. Blood was dripping from the blade. Didn't I already receive a fatal wound...? My mind was hazy as I tried to think. I was losing my sense of reality. Asakura the homicidal maniac. Was that your role here? Yuki Nagato's backup...

And then the knife descended on me...

An arm flashed in from the side.

"—!"

Somebody had grabbed the blade of the knife. Bare-handed.

"Who is it!?" cried Asakura.

Bare-handed...? I feel like I've seen this happen before...

I was unable to recognize the face in my dazed state. There wasn't enough light. Make it brighter. Her face was dark because the streetlight was on the wrong side. A girl with short hair... wearing a North High sailor uniform...no glasses...that was all I could see...Koizumi...can't you do a better job of lighting...?

"Ah...?"

That soft questioning gasp came from Nagato, sitting on the ground. I couldn't see her expression because of the glare on her glasses from the streetlight. Was she scared or surprised...?

"How!? You're...!? Why..."

Asakura was shouting like crazy. She seemed to be talking to whoever had stopped the knife, but that person wasn't answering.

I could hear Asahina's voice nearby.

"I'm sorry...Kyon. I knew this was going to happen..."

"Kyon! Kyon...No! You can't!"

I could see two Asahinas. One was the grown-up Asahina. The other was my childlike Asahina. They were both shaking my body with the same tearful face. Uh, that hurts, you two...?

...Er, why is Asahina (Small) here? I can understand the adult version of Asahina clinging to my body. She came here with me. But where did the small Asahina come from? Oh, I get it. I was either hallucinating or seeing my life flash before my eyes...

The sensation of blood pouring from my body was scarier than any pain I felt.

Crap, I'm gonna die.

As I lamented over how I hadn't prepared any last words, I sensed somebody above my head. That person picked up the Nagato-made injector that had fallen next to me.

And then, in a voice that sounded familiar but that I couldn't recognize...

"Sorry. There's a reason we couldn't save you from that. But don't worry about it. It was a painful experience for me too. Well, we'll manage to take care of the rest. Or yeah, I already know that we're going to take care of the rest. You'll understand soon enough. Just sleep for now."

What are you talking about? Who's doing the talking? What's going on? The images of Asakura's finishing blow, a spectacled Nagato kneeling with her hands on the ground, two Asahinas, and Haruhi wearing a uniform from a different school mixed into a jumbled mess.

And then I blacked out.

CHAPTER 6

Shari shari.

I could hear a crisp sound.

As I began to regain consciousness in the darkness, a corner of my mind was thinking in a daze.

It might have been a dream. You know how when you wake up from an incredible dream, you're all like, wow, for the next five minutes or so, but the details become hazy when you get to brushing your teeth, and by the time you're eating breakfast you've forgotten them entirely. Next thing you know, the impression of an incredible dream is the only thing left. I've experienced that a number of times.

And there were a number of instances in which I could clearly remember every last detail of an incredibly dull dream. Or a dreamlike experience. Like the night when I was stuck in closed space with Haruhi, a memory of an experience that had actually happened before it had been negated.

That was the first thing that came to my mind when I woke up.

I could see a white ceiling. This wasn't my room. It was either morning or dusk, based on the translucent orange glow to the white ceiling and walls.

"Oh!"

That voice sounded as soothing to my still-groggy mind as church bells to devout believers.

"You're finally awake? You seemed to be sound asleep."

I turned my head to look for the person talking. That person was sitting in a chair, next to where I was lying horizontally, peeling an apple with a fruit knife. *Shari shari.* A long piece of red skin dangled without snapping.

"I suppose I should say good morning. Although it's actually evening."

Itsuki Koizumi was sitting there with a gentle smile on his face.

As I watched, Koizumi finished peeling the entire apple and placed it on a plate, which he set down on a side table. Then he drew a second apple from a paper bag before smiling at me.

"It's a good thing you woke up. I was at my wits' end, to be honest. Oh…You seem to be spaced out. Do you recognize me?"

"What about you? Do you know who I am?"

"That's an odd question. Of course I do."

I could tell which Koizumi this was by looking at him.

The dark-blue-blazer school uniform. Not the black traditional one.

It was the North High uniform.

I drew one arm from the blanket covering me. There was an IV drip hooked up to my arm. I stared at it.

"What time is it? What day is it?" I asked.

Koizumi had a look of surprise on his face, or whatever passed as a look of surprise for him.

"That's the first question you have to ask upon waking up? It's almost as if you're aware of your current situation. In any case, the answer would be a little past five PM on December twenty-first."

"The twenty-first, huh...?"

"Yes, three days have passed since you fell unconscious."

Three days? Unconscious?

"Where are we?"

"A private hospital."

I looked at my surroundings. A fancy-looking single room. I was lying on the bed. I was given a private room? I didn't know my family had the money.

"The director of this hospital happens to be an acquaintance of my uncle, so you were provided with special service—that's the story."

Which means it isn't true.

"Yes. I asked the Agency to pull some strings. You'll be able to stay here for an entire year at a cheap price. Having said that, I'm very relieved that you recovered in three days. No, not because of money. My superiors were on my case for letting something happen to you. I had to write up a report."

Three days before the twenty-first would be the eighteenth. What happened to me on that day...? Oh, I see. I almost died from losing too much blood, so they took me to the hospital... no, wait. Something's wrong.

I nervously lifted the hospital gown I was wearing and touched the right side of my body.

Nothing. It didn't hurt or itch at all. That wasn't the kind of wound to heal in three days. Not unless somebody patched me up good.

"Why am I here? You said I was unconscious?"

"So you don't remember? I suppose that's to be expected. You hit your head pretty hard."

I put my hand on my head. I could only feel hair. No bandages or hospital mesh hat.

"That's right. Oddly enough, there wasn't any external sign of injury. No internal bleeding either. And no sign of anything wrong with your brain functions. The doctor couldn't determine what was wrong with you."

Koizumi continued. "However, we all saw you fall down the stairs. That was a dreadful sight. To be honest, it was terrifying to watch. We weren't sure if you'd ever wake up again after hearing you hit the floor so hard. Would you like me to tell you how it happened?"

"Shoot."

I had been going down the stairs in the clubhouse when I either slipped or missed a step. Then I tumbled headfirst with the back of my head hitting the floor with a loud *wham*, and I stopped moving.

That was what had happened, according to Koizumi's explanation.

"It was horrible. We had to call an ambulance and accompany your limp body to the hospital. I'd never seen Suzumiya look so pale before. Oh, Nagato was the one who called for an ambulance. Her ability to keep a cool head may have saved your life."

"How did Asahina react?"

Koizumi shrugged.

"The way you would expect her to react. She was in tears as she clung to your body and cried out your name."

"What time on the eighteenth did it happen? Which floor was I on?"

I fired off questions in rapid succession. The eighteenth would be the first day after the world had changed and left me running around in a panic.

"You don't remember? It was a little after noon. The five of us had just finished an SOS Brigade meeting and were about to go shopping."

Shopping?

"You've lost your memory of that as well? I assume you aren't pretending that you can't remember."

"Just talk."

Koizumi's lips curved into a smile.

"The topic of the meeting that day was, let's see, there will be a party for the children in Suzumiya's neighborhood on the twenty-fifth, Christmas Day, and the SOS Brigade is supposed to make a guest appearance. A way to put Asahina's Santa outfit to good use, I believe. A heartwarming event where she plays Santa and hands out presents to the children. Suzumiya set everything up."

Deciding everything on her own, just as always.

"However, it wouldn't be very realistic if Santa showed up alone, so Suzumiya came up with the idea of Asahina's riding in on somebody in a reindeer costume. We drew lots to determine who would play that role. Well? Are you starting to remember?"

Can't remember a thing. If a guy was able to remember a memory that didn't exist, he'd make a fine swindler. He'd need to check into a different kind of hospital. But there wasn't any point in telling Koizumi this.

"Well, you ended up being picked. So we needed to put together a reindeer costume and we were heading down the stairs of the clubhouse on our way to go buy materials when you fell."

"Sounds dumb."

That drew a frown from Koizumi.

"You were walking at the back of the group. That's why nobody saw what happened. You just came tumbling down," Koizumi said as he dropped the apple from his right hand before catching it in his left, "and flew right past us. However…"

Koizumi returned to peeling the apple.

"After we raced over to your still body, Suzumiya said that she thought she saw someone at the top of the stairs. That she caught a skirt flutter for a moment before it disappeared beyond the corner of the landing. I was curious, so I asked around, but we were the only ones in the clubhouse at the time, and Nagato also shook her head. A phantom girl. We were waiting for you to tell us if you were pushed off or not…"

Don't remember. That would be the best response. Just an accident. An unfortunate accident brought about by my carelessness. I'll go with that.

"Are you the only one who's come to visit?"

"What about Haruhi?" would have been the next words out of my mouth, but I stopped myself. However, Koizumi still chuckled.

"You keep glancing around. Are you looking for someone in particular? There's no need to worry. We've been taking turns watching over you so there would be someone around when you woke up. Asahina should be coming soon."

Koizumi gave me a funny look. The look you'd give a friend who completely fell for an April Fools' joke, while laughing at him on the inside. What was that look for?

"No, I was just feeling a bit jealous. Or envious, if you please."

Kind of odd for you to feel that way, considering the circumstances.

"The brigade members have been rotating shifts, but it's apparently part of the brigade chief's job to worry about the health of her subordinates."

Koizumi began methodically slicing the peeled apples and shaping the slices into rabbits before placing them on a plate on the table.

"Suzumiya has been here the entire time. The entire three days."

I looked in the direction he was pointing. The side of the bed opposite Koizumi. On the floor.

"…"

There she was.

Haruhi was sleeping snugly in a sleeping bag with her mouth in an upside-down V.

"We were very worried. Both she and I."

He was laying it on thick with the mournful tone.

"Suzumiya was especially upset...well, I can tell you about that at a later date. In any case, you have something else to do first, right?"

Everybody likes to boss me around. Asahina (Big), Koizumi... But I'm not going to say anything about that. I didn't care whom those extra peeled apples were for.

"Right," I said.

Draw on her face...or no. I can do that some other time. There'll be plenty of chances for that.

I stretched my arm out from its position on the bed and touched her angry-looking face with my fingertips.

Hair that wasn't long enough for a ponytail. A painfully familiar sight. Her black hair shook in a teasing way.

Haruhi opened her eyes.

"...Uh?"

Haruhi peered at me with bleary eyes as she groaned before finally realizing who was pinching her cheek.

"Ah!"

She apparently forgot that she was in a sleeping bag. Her attempt to spring up failed as she fell down and wriggled around like an inchworm before somehow managing to stand up and stab a finger in my face while shouting.

"Stupid Kyon! If you're awake, then tell me that you're awake before waking me up! I have to prepare myself!"

Don't be ridiculous. Still, your loud voice is better than any medicine right now.

"Haruhi."

"What!?"

"Wipe your drool."

Haruhi rubbed at her mouth as her lips and eyebrows twitched. She rubbed her entire face while glaring at me.

"You didn't draw on my face, did you?"

I was tempted.

"Hmph. So, don't you have anything else to say to me?"

I gave her the reply she wanted.

"I guess I gave you all a scare. Sorry about that."

"A-as long as you understand. Of course. It's part of the brigade chief's job to worry about brigade members!"

Haruhi's yelling was sweet music to my ears. I heard a soft knock on the door. Koizumi stood up tactfully and pulled the sliding door open.

There stood the third visitor, who took one look at me and lost her calm.

"Ah. Ah, ah…"

The short and lovely North High upperclassman, a miraculous fusion of soft hair and doll face, stood in the entrance carrying a vase.

"Hey…Asahina. Hi there."

I wasn't exactly sure how long it'd been since we last met.

"Wah…"

Tears began to trickle down Asahina's face.

"Thank heaven…Really…I'm so glad…"

I would have loved for her to throw herself into my arms again, and Asahina seemed ready to do just that, but she had forgotten to set the vase down, so she just stood there and cried.

"You're overreacting. He just hit his head and passed out. I knew all along that Kyon would wake up eventually."

Haruhi sounded a little jittery as she spoke without looking at me.

"Because I already decided that the SOS Brigade runs year-round without any breaks. Every one of us has to be on the job. A hard knock to the head or a coma won't be an acceptable excuse. Understand? Kyon, going AWOL for three days comes with a heavy price. You get a penalty! A penalty! Plus interest!"

Koizumi was smiling pleasantly as Asahina continued to rain large teardrops onto the floor and Haruhi looked away from me in a huff.

I looked across all of them before nodding and shrugging.

"I know. So, with interest, how much do I owe you?"

Haruhi glared at me before bursting into a surreal smile. She's so simpleminded.

I was told that I'd be paying for everybody at the café for three days. I'll probably have to withdraw my savings.

"And…"

There's more?

"Yep, you have to pay separately for the emotional stress you caused everyone. That's right, Kyon. At the Christmas party, you have to wear the reindeer costume and perform something for us. You'll have to keep going until you've managed to thoroughly entertain every one of us. I'll kick you into another dimension if it's boring! And you'll have to perform for the children too. Understood!?"

Haruhi's eyes were shining like prisms as she stabbed her finger at me again.

I'd managed to regain consciousness, but I couldn't be discharged from the hospital right away. After a doctor raced over to ask me

some questions, I was taken to an examination room and put through all kinds of machines. It was so bad that I was wondering if they were trying to turn me into a cyborg. And since they blew the entire day running checkups and various tests, I had to spend another night in the hospital. Though it was really the first night for me and I'd never been hospitalized before, so this was an interesting experience.

Haruhi, along with Koizumi and Asahina, apparently just missed my mother and sister on their way out. I suppose they were trying to be considerate, in which case I'd be amazed by the fact that Haruhi knew how to be considerate.

While my sister and mother chatted, I pondered the recent events.

What would have happened if I had left everything the way it was? Nagato, Asahina, and Koizumi would be ordinary humans without any supernatural identities. Nagato would be a reticent book-loving literary club member, Asahina would be an upper-classman out of reach, and Koizumi would be a normal transfer student at a different school.

And Haruhi would just be a girl in high school with a slightly twisted personality.

That could have been the beginning of a new story. A story about an everyday life that had nothing to do with facing reality or how the world was supposed to be.

I probably wouldn't have any role to play in that story. I would go through high school without any incident and graduate without any incident.

Which world would I be happier with?

I already knew the answer.

The "present" was more fun. Otherwise, my near-death experience would have been for nothing, right?

Here's a question. Which would you choose? The answer should be obvious. Or am I the only one who feels this way?

Eventually my family left, and it was time to turn off the lights in my hospital room. I had nothing to do as I stared at the ceiling, so I closed my eyes and sought darkness.

My past three days. In this world, I'd been asleep for the past three days, apparently.

In that case—

The world had to be altered for that to be true.

This world had been altered twice. The other Nagato's twisted world had been retransformed into the original world, the one I was in now. So who was responsible for the second retransformation?

It wasn't Haruhi. The Haruhi from those three days had no power and this Haruhi didn't know that the world had been changed.

So who did it?

The person who stopped Asakura's flashing knife bare-handed, someone capable of such a thing, someone willing to do such a thing—

It could only be Nagato.

And I had seen two Asahinas before I lost consciousness. The Asahina who wasn't grown-up. That had been my Asahina, the one in this world. The lovely upperclassman from the future who I knew so well.

And there was one more person, the one who had spoken. The one who talked to me at the end in a strangely familiar voice.

I struggled to place that voice before I soon realized that there wasn't any need.

That was my voice.

—I see. That's what happened.

So basically.

I would have to go back to that time again. I would have to travel through time and arrive early in the morning on December eighteenth. With the Asahina and Nagato from this time.

That would restore the world to its current state.

Asahina's role would be to take Nagato and me to that time. Nagato's role would be to normalize the crazed three-day period and crazed Nagato. Though I didn't know if she would be borrowing Haruhi's power again or if the Data Overmind would handle it.

And I also had a role to play.

I mean, right? I heard my own voice at the time. That was part of the reason why I'm here right now. I needed to go back to the past and say something to myself so I could exist.

"Sorry. There's a reason we couldn't save you from that. But don't worry about it. It was a painful experience for me too. Well, we'll manage to take care of the rest. Or yeah, I already know that we're going to take care of the rest. You'll understand soon enough. Just sleep for now."

I practiced my lines. Pretty sure that was how it went. Not sure if I got every word right, but it was probably close enough.

It would be my job to use the injector in place of the me who had been felled by an assassin's dagger.

I could also understand why nobody had saved me from the psycho Asakura. Judging from my voice, I hadn't raced over to myself because I'd been hiding somewhere nearby. I, along with Asahina and Nagato, had been waiting for the right time to show ourselves. We didn't want to be too early or too late. I had to be stabbed by Asakura. Because for the other me there at that time, it was something that had already happened in his past. Or, as Asahina would put it—

"Established information."

*　　*　　*

It was getting late in the night, but I still didn't feel like going to sleep.

I was waiting. Waiting for what? That should be obvious. There was one more person who was supposed to show up but hadn't. Someone who was a guaranteed lock to come.

I lay down on the bed and stared at the ceiling. My patience wasn't rewarded until the dead of night. Long past visiting hours.

The door to my room slowly slid open as the shadow of a small figure in the hallway extended across the floor.

The last person to visit me that day was Yuki Nagato in her sailor uniform.

Nagato was stone-faced as always.

"All responsibility lies with me."

It was very reassuring to hear her flat voice for what felt like the first time in ages.

"Punitive measures are being evaluated."

I lifted my head.

"By who?"

"The Data Overmind."

Nagato continued in her flat voice, as though none of this concerned her:

Naturally, Nagato knew what she had done in the early morning of December eighteenth because the grown-up Asahina and I had gone to visit Nagato three years ago. She had known what would happen and done her best to avoid this outcome. But she couldn't. There are times when you can know what's going to happen in the future and still be unable to avoid it. No, if that were the case…

I suddenly recalled how Nagato seemed to be acting differently after the summer.

"In that case," I interjected, "you would have known three years ago that you were going to bug out. In that case, you could have told me about this at any time, right? After the cultural festival or before the baseball game, even. I would have been able to act faster on December eighteenth then. Assemble all the members and go three years back in time."

Nagato's face was grim, as though incapable of smiling.

"Even if I were to have communicated that information to you beforehand, I would have erased all corresponding memories upon malfunctioning and proceeded to alter the world. Again, there is no guarantee that the above did not happen. I could only manage to preserve your original state when the eighteenth arrived."

"You also left the escape program, right? That was enough."

As I thanked her, I began to feel irritated. Not because of Nagato. Not because of me either.

Her flat voice echoed softly in the hospital room.

"There is no guarantee that I will not malfunction again. As long as I continue to exist, internal errors will continue to accumulate. The possibility remains. A significant risk."

"Tell them to go suck it."

Nagato responded to that curse by silently lowering her head two millimeters. Her eyes blinked.

I reached out with my arm to take her thin and pale hand. Nagato didn't resist.

"Tell your boss. If you leave or disappear, okay? I'll go crazy. I'll do anything to take you back. I don't personally have any special powers, but I'm able to set Haruhi loose."

I happen to hold the key for doing that. All I have to do is say, "I'm John Smith," and that's that.

Yeah, that's right. I have as much power as a loofah. However, Haruhi has as much power as a giant oak tree. If Nagato were to disappear, I'd tell her everything and convince her to believe me. And then we would head out to find Nagato. It wouldn't matter what Nagato's boss had done to hide or eliminate her. Haruhi would find a way. I would make it happen. And I might as well get Koizumi and Asahina involved. Who cares about some discarnate data entity that's off somewhere in the universe? Screw that.

Nagato was one of us. And Haruhi would be the last person to ever give up if someone in the SOS Brigade were to go missing. This wasn't limited to Nagato. If Koizumi, Asahina, or I were to run off, even if we were to go willingly, she would never accept that. I guarantee that she would do whatever it took to bring us back. That's how Haruhi Suzumiya was. Our selfish and self-centered troublemaking brigade chief who couldn't be bothered to consider other people.

I gave Nagato a hard look.

"If any of you try to argue, I'll join Haruhi in remaking the world. Into a world like the one I just spent three days in, where your Data Overmind no longer exists. That'll leave you all in despair. So much for observing. How do you like that?"

I was starting to get really pissed.

I didn't care about how advanced the Data Overmind was. Probably had plenty of brains. Enough to calculate pi to the trillionth digit within a couple of seconds. Probably capable of all sorts of fancy tricks.

So then, my point was:

You could have given Yuki Nagato an actual personality. You could have made her into something like pre-homicidal-maniac Asakura, someone cheerful and sociable who was popular with classmates and goes shopping with friends at the mall on weekends. Why did you turn her into a gloomy girl who spent her time cooped up inside and reading all alone? Because that was expected from a member of the literary club? Whose idea was it?

I came to my senses as I realized that I was tightly gripping Nagato's hand. However, the book-loving organic android didn't say anything.

Nagato simply stared at me before slowly nodding.

"I will tell them."

Her voice was still flat as she murmured, "Thank you."

EPILOGUE

Well, I thought.

Closing ceremonies were over and homeroom teacher Okabe had handed out report cards. That ended my high school life for the year.

Today's date was December twenty-fourth.

The members of 1-9 who had disappeared with their classroom were back and Koizumi, who hadn't played much of a role this time, was also there. Asakura had disappeared from class 1-5 over half a year ago. Taniguchi was still in a celebratory mood. Haruhi was still positioned in the seat behind mine. There was no flu epidemic at our school. When I saw Nagato in the auditorium she wasn't wearing glasses, and when I happened to run into the Asahina/Tsuruya duo after the closing ceremony, they both said hi. And on my way to school I'd checked to see that the private Kouyouen Academy was once again a school for rich high-society girls.

The world was back to normal.

However, I still had a choice to make. Nagato, Asahina, and I would have to return to the past—early in the morning on

December eighteenth—again to preserve the restored world. That trip was what turned everything back to normal. However, I haven't decided when to go. I haven't told Asahina about any of this yet. I doubt that she'd heard anything from the adult version of herself. From what I've seen over the past few days, she doesn't have a clue.

"Man."

I sighed for no reason and stepped into the corridor that led to the clubhouse.

Maybe there was a rule in place that I had to keep returning to the same point, like a race car on a closed circuit. The second and third laps wouldn't feel very different. Even if they did, it wasn't for me to decide. The opening and final laps would be set on the exact same path with the exact same scenery, yet hold completely different meanings. I just had to make my way to the finish line while being careful to avoid elimination. Yes, until the checkered flag came down.

…Well, I realize that I'm going overboard with this line of reasoning.

It was useless to try to make excuses, because I had chosen this world. This wasn't like when Haruhi went on a merry rampage unconsciously. I had consciously chosen to live in a world where we ran in circles while making a mess.

In that case, I had an obligation to see things through.

Not Nagato. Not Haruhi. It was my responsibility, now that I'd thrown my lot in with them.

"Serves me right, huh?"

I tried to knock myself off my high horse. The end result was rather ugly, but I didn't really care. Nobody was watching. Or so I thought when my eyes met the eyes of a nameless female student. She quickly looked away and scurried off as I watched.

"Merry Christmas Eve," I said softly, in a voice that couldn't be heard.

If this were the last episode of a hackneyed TV drama, a white flake would come fluttering down and land in my palm as I gasped, but it seems that we weren't meant to have a white Christmas. It was an incredibly sunny day.

I placed my foot on the first step.

I had been completely transformed into an interested party. My role as an innocent bystander was a relic of the past, banished to the depths of the galaxy.

"So what?"

What was the point in realizing this now? I was one of them. I knew that a long time ago. After Haruhi dragged me to the literary club room and declared that she was taking it over.

Like the other members of the SOS Brigade, I was on the side that was actively protecting this world. And I hadn't been pushed into this. I voluntarily raised my hand.

As I climbed the stairs, I switched to thinking about the event that was scheduled to begin soon. Haruhi and Asahina had done the shopping in the end. I'd been excused from my assigned role of carrying stuff, since I was fresh out of the hospital. Though this really wasn't an example of Haruhi's being considerate, since her goal was to hide the menu until the very last second so she could surprise everyone—at least, that was her plan. She might be attempting to use her experience from the remote island. An economical mystery pot Christmas party.

What would we find inside? Knowing Haruhi, her priority was to surprise, so we might end up with some kind of experimental and bizarre hot pot, the like of which hasn't occurred in the history of mankind. Still, most stuff was edible if you boiled it long enough. Haruhi wasn't going to throw in anything that her own stomach wouldn't be able to digest, unless she had the stomach of a monster. But I would assume that Haruhi, master of defying common sense, still had a stomach that conformed to human standards. The only part of her that's transcended human norms would be whatever's inside her head.

And I was supposed to perform in the reindeer costume as a sort of sideshow to the hot-pot party. Try to consider how hard it was for me to come up with material to work with.

"Good grief."

I voiced the interjection I had determined to seal away last month, but yeah, whatever. The words may have sounded the same, but they might as well have been completely different words, since the meaning was different.

And with that follow-up explanation, I added an item to my mental schedule book.

That item was *established information*. Something I absolutely had to do to remain here in this present.

—I would have to go restore this world in the near future.

As I approached the clubroom, a fragrant aroma tickled the mucous membranes of my nose. That was enough to make me feel like my stomach was full, but I had to wonder why there was a sense of satisfaction. I still needed to travel through time soon. It was too early to feel satisfied.

—But, yeah. Before that.

There was still time. A future version of me would be handling that. Not that it would happen in the distant future, but it wouldn't come in the immediate future.

As I placed my hand on the literary club room doorknob, I posed a question to the world.

Hey, world. Could you wait a bit? Hold on a little longer until I go to retransform you.

—I mean.

I should at least have time to enjoy Haruhi's special hot pot, right?

AFTERWORD

I hope you'll forgive my relating an old memory in place of an afterword.

When I was in sixth grade, there was a boy in my class who was literally a genius. He was a central figure in our class with a sharp mind and good family background who was also gentle, with a smile that could brighten a room. He was shining with charisma. I happened to become friends with this boy because we shared the same interests. Fishing and foreign mystery novels. I wouldn't know how to rate that combination.

I was also assigned to the same group as him. Naturally, he was the leader of the group. Once there was an event in which a group from every class was supposed to perform before the entire grade. Our group was running out of time to decide on a performance when he said, "Let's do a play," and wrote an original script. I'll never forget it. I was rolling around on the floor laughing with tears in my eyes as I read his script. I didn't know it was possible for something so funny to exist.

And we were able to faithfully perform that scenario under his direction. Our play had the sixth graders laughing. Even the teachers were laughing. Our group won the gold award and a wooden shield. I can still remember the role I played as though it happened yesterday.

After that I enjoyed middle school with him before he went on to a high school far away, and a college that was even farther away.

At times I would wonder if I could ever make people laugh the way he did—and if his script had flipped a switch somewhere in my mind—

That feeling took root in my mind and became an unforgettable memory.

…Guess that wasn't long enough. I'll continue with a second memory.

In high school, I was a member of the literary club for a brief moment. I mainly focused on a different club, so I only went to the literary club once a week, if that. However, the club only met once a week to begin with. The first time I knocked on the door, I was greeted by an intelligent-looking girl with glasses who happened to be the only member, the president of the club, and an upperclassman. I can't remember if I said anything or if I even had anything to say. It's entirely possible that we never spoke at all.

After I joined the club, the two of us made a literary club magazine. I'd rather not remember what I wrote at the time. Not a story. I also drew the cover. Don't want to remember that either. The two of us couldn't fill all the pages by ourselves, so she asked a number of her friends to contribute articles. On an unrelated note, one of those friends had a very striking name that I can still remember.

Once that upperclassman was a senior, she quit the club to focus on her studies. At the same time, around five new members joined. Not sure why. I was having much more fun in my other club, so I soon stopped going to the literary club.

I ran into that upperclassman on the day she graduated. I don't remember what we talked about. We probably just chatted idly for a bit before I watched her leave.

I can't remember the name of that upperclassman. I'm sure that she doesn't remember my name either. But I would hope that she remembers the existence of such a person at the time.

The way I do.

…And so I more or less filled up the afterword with a couple sonnets about painful memories that don't sound very real, but I have to admit that when I dug through my hazy memories, there were many more headaches than humorous episodes, enough to make me swoon…I'd find myself wondering if I could have handled something better, but that would accomplish about as much as wondering about the fate of a soccer ball floating down a river. I should probably focus on something else.

Finally, I would like to offer a dance of gratitude to the publishers of this book, along with the readers. Until next time.

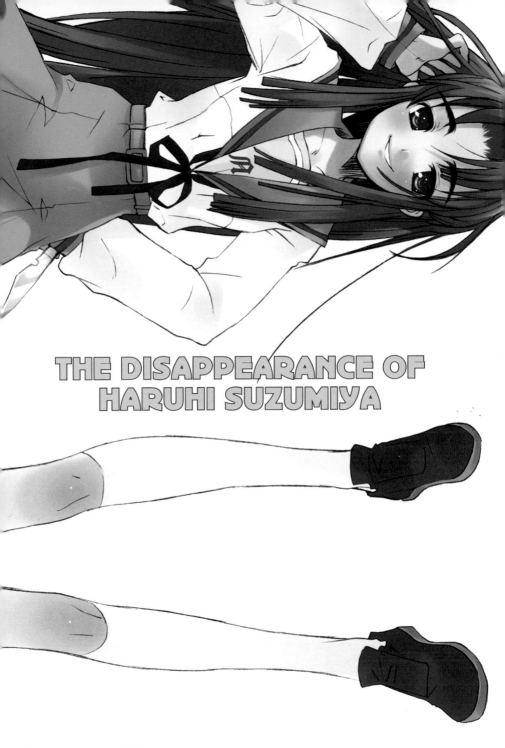

THE DISAPPEARANCE OF
HARUHI SUZUMIYA

Illustration by Noizi ITO

I WAS HANDED A BLANK
APPLICATION FORM.
IF YOU'D LIKE . . .